A Girl Called
Rosemary

A Girl Called Rosemary

by Dianne Doubtfire

SCHOLASTIC BOOK SERVICES
New York Toronto London Auckland Sydney Tokyo

Copyright © 1977 Dianne Doubtfire. All rights re-
served. Published by Scholastic Book Services, a division
of Scholastic Magazines, Inc.

12 11 10 9 8 7 6 5 4 3   7 8 9/7 0 1 2/8

Chapter 1

"Where's Leo?" Aunt Kay's shrill voice echoed up the stairs. Rosemary caught her breath and said nothing.

"Rosemary! Do you hear me? Are you in your room?"

Rosemary winced as if she'd been pricked with a needle. "Yeah — I'm here."

"Where's Leo?" The voice was nearer, sharper. Aunt Kay must be coming up the plushy red stairs in her bedroom slippers.

"Dunno." Rosemary went on drawing. It was another of her wallpaper designs and she outlined a sunflower over and over again so that the pencil nearly went through the paper. She knew very well that her brother was hiding in the coalshed but she wasn't

1

going to betray him. Leo was eleven, four years younger than Rosemary. She had seen him vanish into the black, cobwebby doorway a few minutes earlier. He had spotted her at the bedroom window, grinned up at her, then pressed his finger to his mouth with an urgent "shushing" expression before he disappeared. Rosemary knew why he was hiding; it was time to get ready for Sunday School.

Leo had fallen out with God since his parents were killed in an air crash that spring. "How could He let them die when they were so *good*?" he would cry. "How could He let *them* die and let bad people go on living?" Rosemary couldn't bear to see his round, freckled face distorted with such grief. Before they were killed, his young life had brimmed with enjoyment. His father had been wild and adventurous and full of fun, his mother gentle and kind. Apart from whooping cough and the death of his kitten there had been nothing for Leo to worry about. Now, in place of his mother there was this domineering aunt, his mother's sister, and for a foster-father the gray, abstracted Uncle Bert who worked in a tax office and spent all his spare time in the attic with a collection of old musical instruments.

Aunt Kay opened the door of Rosemary's room and walked in. "It's time that boy was ready for Sunday School," she said irritably, marching across to the open window. She put her head out and shouted "Leo!" in a high-pitched screech.

Rosemary couldn't help smiling to herself as she pictured Leo's bright mischievous eyes in the gloom of the coalshed. There was no reply, no sound but the hum of traffic on the main road and the distant squealing of sea-gulls in the clear August sky. Rosemary and Leo now lived with their aunt and uncle in Brinely, a busy seaside town in the south of England. From the attic, if you pushed past the array of cellos and harps and mandolins to the dusty little window, you could just catch a glimpse of the sea, a narrow glitter between the chimneys and television aerials. Living at the seaside had been the one good thing to come out of the tragedy. Their old home had been in London.

Now Aunt Kay was examining her face in the wardrobe mirror. She was a trim, good-looking woman but her nose and chin were sharp and her hair was done in stiff lac-quered curls like scrolls of brass. She and Bert had no children of their own and Rose-mary felt sure they hadn't really wanted her and Leo; it had been a duty they couldn't escape and they were trying to make the best of it.

"This eye shadow's too blue," announced

3

Aunt Kay. "My eyes are green. Don't you think they're green?"

Rosemary shook back her long hair and looked at her aunt's eyes. They were a strange color, and without sparkle, like an icy pond. Her mother's eyes had been gray like her own.

"Yeah — sort of greenish," she said.

There was a silence while Rosemary went back to her drawing. Her hair fell heavily forward, hanging round her small face like a curtain. Aunt Kay was still peering into the mirror.

Then Rosemary said, "I don't think he wants to go."

"Who doesn't want to go where?"

"Leo. He doesn't want to go to Sunday School."

"Well, if he doesn't go he'll get no pocket money next week."

Rosemary knew this would be a shock for him. He was saving every penny for a big model racing car he'd seen in a shop in the town. Leo was crazy about cars. Maybe I ought to warn him, she thought. Aunt Kay was still absorbed by her reflection and Rosemary put down her drawing book and sauntered out of the room.

The staircase was steep and the red carpet so thick you had to be careful not to slip. Out in the small back yard, below her bedroom window, she stopped by the coalshed and pretended to blow her nose.

"Leo!" she whispered into her handkerchief. "She's stopping your money if you don't go."

There was a faint answering groan and a moment later Leo came scrambling out of the shed onto the concrete path, his carrotty hair on end and his round face streaked with coal dust. He was a tough, stocky little lad with big goldy-brown eyes and pale brows and lashes. He squirmed as Rosemary dusted the cobwebs off his blue T-shirt and jeans.

"Be careful," she muttered. "She's in my room."

"What do I care?"

"You'd better get washed and ready if you don't want to lose your pocket money."

Leo looked up at his sister and his mouth was tight with defiance. "I'm not going," he said. "If she won't give me my money I'll get it somehow else."

"Leo — what do you mean?" Rosemary frowned at him anxiously.

"You'll see." He took a step nearer. "I've got a new friend. I met him yesterday in The Winner and his name's Derek Halsey and he said I could call him Hal. He's sixteen."

The Winner was an amusement arcade on the Promenade. Rosemary had never won anything there but she'd seen Leo topple a pile of coins into the chute by giving the machine a mighty heave with his hard little shoulder when no one was looking.

"You won't get the money for your car in The Winner," she said drily. "I can promise you that."

"I didn't say I would. I didn't *say* that, did I? I said I'd get it somehow else. You'll see."

"You wouldn't steal, would you, Leo?"

He shook his head. "Course not."

She believed him. "Come on," she coaxed. "Get yourself cleaned up and go and tell Aunt Kay you're ready. You've just got time."

"No, I'm not going."

"Come on — it doesn't take much."

"It *does* — it *does* take much!" His mouth was no longer grim; it was soft and wobbly. Rosemary guessed he was thinking of those Sunday afternoons when their parents were alive. There had been no Sunday School, but the hours had been crowded with warmth and fun and absorbing activities. Now there was only this cold unfeeling aunt, forcing her nephew to learn about a God he no longer trusted. Rosemary understood and she was on Leo's side.

"O.K.," she said, ruffling his spiky hair. "O.K. — go off and play!"

He ran out of the gate without looking at her, and she heard him racing down the street. Off to look for Hal, no doubt . . .

She walked slowly back to the house and when she reached her room she was startled to find her aunt still there; she was sitting on a chair by the window and her face was stiff with anger.

"I heard that, Rosemary. I heard you tell your brother to go off and play when he ought to be at Sunday School. You're as bad as he is, encouraging him to disobey me. I don't know what your mother would have thought — she'd have been *ashamed* of you, wouldn't she?"

Rosemary stared at her aunt for a moment of helpless misery and then she burst out, "No — she wouldn't — she'd have understood. She *always* understood!"

She ran out of the house, stumbling over the doorstep, slamming the garden gate. She kept on walking until she reached a huge car dump — hundreds of battered old vehicles left to rust among the brambles and bindweed. She sat on a pile of rotting motor tires and let the tears come flooding down her cheeks.

Chapter 2

The Winner was a square brick building
with a yellow flag on top. It was close to the
sea, at the slummy end of the Promenade,
and on this Sunday afternoon the flag was
fluttering sleepily in the warm breeze. As
soon as Leo caught sight of it, he began to
run as fast as he could, weaving his way
among the pavement crowds. He wanted to
find Hal but he was half afraid of seeing him
again in case he had changed his mind.

The Winner was dazzlingly bright inside
and he felt very small among the big lads in
their jeans or smart suits and the tall girls
with their cool faces and painted eyes. Some
of the girls wore long skirts and some wore
scanty beach clothes but they all seemed

strange and distant and not a bit like Rosemary. He was nervous of girls, except for his sister. The air smelled of smoke and scent and sweat and orange peel, and the thump of the juke-box was almost drowned by the clatter of the games and machines, the laughter and talk, the tramp of feet.

Suddenly Leo caught sight of Hal at a pinball machine. He recognized him from behind by his long blond hair and the black leather jacket with "H" on the back in brass studs.

"Hi, Hal!"

Hal swung round, frowning, until he saw it was Leo. Then he smiled broadly, his teeth large and even, like false ones.

"If it isn't young Leo! I thought you had to go to Sunday School."

"Well, I didn't, did I? I came here instead."

Hal frowned again. He was a good-looking boy but when he scowled he looked quite ugly. "Does that mean you want to go ahead with that business deal?"

Leo nodded. The words "business deal" gave him a thrill of excitement. He hoped he'd be able to measure up to Hal's requirements as a partner. Hal was just the kind of friend he wanted — strong, and confident, and daring, like his father. Besides, he needed the bread for that model racing car. He wasn't going to be dependent on Aunt Kay's whims for his spending money.

Hal put his hand on Leo's shoulder and pushed him gently towards the exit. "We'll go somewhere quiet and I'll tell you what you've got to do," he said. "Only don't forget what I told you yesterday. It's *secret*. You're not to tell *anyone* — and if you do you'll be sorry —"

"I won't tell," said Leo. He was good at keeping secrets. Rosemary had often confided in him and he had never given her away.

"You've got to *swear*," said Hal as they headed for a flight of stone steps that led down to the beach. "You've got to swear on your own blood."

Leo felt a pang in his stomach but he said nothing. He took a deep breath and looked at Hal, who had paused to light a cigarette and now tossed the empty packet onto the pavement.

"Litter-lout," said Leo.

Hal took hold of Leo's ear and pinched it so hard that he nearly cried out. "What did you say?"

"I said 'litter-lout.' That's what my mother used to call me if I threw paper down in the street."

"Well, don't you call me names! If we're working together like I said, *I'm* the one that gives the orders and you do exactly as you're told."

"Why?" Leo stared up steadily into Hal's

hostile face, holding his gaze but quaking at the knees.

"For one thing, I'm five years older than you are. For another thing, the whole scheme is *my* idea. And for another thing, if you don't want to take orders from me you can clear off and be quick about it. I can soon find someone else to be my partner."

Leo stood firmly where he was but now he avoided Hal's eyes because his lips were feeling quivery. He pulled a piece of bubble-gum out of the pocket of his jeans, inspected it for fluff, and put it into his mouth, chewing strongly.

Hal bent down and thrust his face close to Leo's. His eyes were bright blue with long curling lashes like a girl's. His cheeks and top lip were covered with pale downy hair which made Leo envious because his own freckled cheeks were smooth and shiny.

"Are you going then?" said Hal. "Because if you are, get out this minute. Go on, get out!"

Leo shook his head and chewed bravely into that handsome, menacing face. "I'm not going," he said. "I'll be your partner."

Hal straightened and smiled his slow charming smile. The breeze lifted his yellow hair and blew it across his face as he turned away, drawing on his cigarette. "All right then. We'll go down onto the beach and I'll swear you in. I've got a knife."

"What knife?" Leo felt sick.

"To swear you in. On your own blood. You said you wanted to be my partner."

"Yeah. Yeah — I do." His heart was thumping.

Hal marched ahead and began to descend the stone steps. They led down to a dirty patch of beach, stinking with seaweed and littered with tin cans, plastic bottles, and all kinds of débris. There was a red sandal, a battered pair of headphones, a sodden magazine . . .

Hal leapt down the last three steps and stood triumphantly among the jetsam, facing Leo. "Come on. Not chicken are you?"

Leo stopped and blew his bubble-gum out into a vast balloon. Then he sucked it in, took it out of his mouth and stuck it on the handrail that ran beside the steps. He grinned. "Somebody's going to get a nice surprise," he said.

Hal didn't smile. "Come on," he snapped. "I haven't got all day."

Leo joined him. There was no one else on that dirty stretch of beach. A seagull stood preening itself on a rock, and the waves broke lazily, shifting the rubbish at the water's edge into new positions.

Leo said, "Where are you going to cut me?"

"I'm not going to cut you. You have to do it yourself."

Leo gulped with relief. Maybe that wouldn't be so bad. He'd do it on his leg — just a little nick. But he quailed at the thought of it.

Hal took a penknife out of an inside pocket and opened it carefully. Then suddenly he threw it to Leo. "Here — catch!"

Leo put out his hand to intercept it as it whizzed through the air and caught it just before it hit the ground.

He held it up to Hal, laughing. The blood was running across the palm of his hand and he felt no pain, only a marvelous sense of joy that the ordeal was over for him so quickly and unexpectedly. "There you are," he cried. "Plenty of blood! Now what do you want me to swear? Come on, I haven't got all day!"

Hal frowned for an instant, then he smiled. "You're a good kid. Here — have you got a handkerchief?"

Leo shook his head, and as he sat beside his new friend on the pebbly beach among the refuse, allowing him to wrap a grubby handkerchief round his small, bleeding hand, he felt happier than he had felt for months.

"Thank you for letting me be your business partner, Hal," he said.

Chapter 3

Rosemary felt better when she had finished crying. She wiped her eyes on the hem of her pink cotton dress and looked around at the deserted car dump. A wilderness of discarded vehicles stretched as far as she could see, humps of rusted rooftops huddled among the undergrowth like dead or dying animals. That's what they are, in a way, she thought. They used to have warm, throbbing hearts and race along so fast and free; now they're lifeless. She loved motors, as Leo did, and she hated to see those derelict bodies, the great headlamp eyes, now blind forever, the wheels that would never turn again . . . Suddenly she caught sight of a boy leaning over an old blue car some distance away, near the entrance to the dump. He was tugging at something, trying to detach it from the car.

Rosemary was intrigued and walked casually back towards the main road. When she approached the boy, she saw he was in fact a young man of about eighteen, rather fat, with a rosy face and black curly hair. He was trying to get a side-mirror free, but without success. As she passed him, he glanced up and smiled.

Rosemary stopped. It might have been his friendly face or her own loneliness, but somehow she knew she had to talk to him.

"Can I help?" she said.

"'Fraid not — unless you've got a wrench in your pocket!" He grinned at her, still tugging at the mirror, twisting it this way and that. "I thought it might have rusted loose but it hasn't."

"Was it your car?"

"Lord, no — I'm at the Polytechnic — starving on a grant. I wanted a mirror for my room and I saw this flashing in the sun. It was beckoning me!"

Rosemary smiled. She liked that — it tied up with her own idea of cars with a life of their own. "Are you allowed to take things off these motors, then?" She was wondering what she might find for her own room; it was fun scavenging.

"Dunno. I expect it's all right — no use to anyone now, are they?" He began pulling at the mirror again.

"I suppose there wouldn't be a wrench left behind in the trunk?" she suggested. There had always been tools in the back of her father's car.

He laughed. It was a loud bubbly laugh, but not the kind that makes you feel a fool. "I think that would be asking *too* much, but there's no harm in looking." He straightened and she saw that he wasn't much taller than herself.

They went to the back of the car, pushing aside the brambles, and she watched as he wrenched at the rusty handle. In a few moments the whole lid came off in one simple movement as if it was made of cardboard. The hinges had rusted to powder and a shower of red dust scattered over his shoes as the crumbling lid fell into the long grass.

It was then that Rosemary let out a gasp of horror. Lying on its side in the trunk was the corpse of a black and white fox terrier.

Rosemary turned away, sick with pity and revulsion.

"Been dead ages, by the look of it," said the boy. "Lord, what a stink!"

"How could anybody *do* such a thing?" choked Rosemary. "What a horrible way for the poor thing to die."

"Might have been dead before they put it in there," he said. "Might've been knocked down by a car and died in a flash. So don't worry."

"You can't be sure."

"No, but if you don't *know* how it happened, why not imagine the best, not the worst?"

Rosemary looked at him and met his dark-brown friendly eyes. "I'm glad you said that," she told him. "I'm *terribly* glad you said that!"

He looked puzzled. "Good. But why?"

"My parents were killed in an air crash last April and I don't know *how* they died — if it was quick — or not. I've kept thinking awful things — the very worst — and I can see that's wrong. It *might* have been quick."

He nodded gravely. "Course it might. Most likely was. Poor you, that was tough."

"Yeah."

He turned back to look at the dog and Rosemary now had the courage to look again herself. Already a drift of flies was hovering round the small matted corpse.

The boy picked up the trunk lid and set it roughly in place, covering the dog. "I'll bury it," he said. "I'll go home for a spade and bury it here, by the car."

Rosemary thought, He's just the sort of boy I could really like. Nothing special to look at but really sweet. "My name's Rose-mary," she said. "Rosemary Carter. What's yours?"

"Scott Fleming. Are you on holiday?"

"No, I live near the Roxy Cinema with my aunt and uncle. And my kid brother."

"I bet you miss your parents," he said.

Surprisingly, she was able to answer without a tremor. "I expect I'll get over it in time." She smiled at him.

"Were they good parents?"

Now the tears welled up. She couldn't speak, only nod vigorously.

"My father died three years ago," he said, "and my mother doesn't really *want* to get over it. She won't have him mentioned — it's all wrong. He was great, too — they were really happy. I want to *talk* about him — just normally — but she won't have it. And I've got no brothers or sisters so I have to keep it bottled up."

"You can talk about him to me," said Rosemary.

"Thanks," he said. "And you must tell me about your parents as well." He wiped his hands on his white jeans, leaving smears of red rust down both sides. "Come and have some tea at the Wimpy," he said. "I can bury this poor little wretch this evening."

"I'll help you."

"Great."

They walked out of the car dump in silence. It was an easy silence, not the sort that makes you feel as if you ought to think of something to say.

When Rosemary saw the yellow flag of The Winner waving against the blue sky, she remembered Leo. She hoped he had managed to find Hal; he needed a friend, an older boy who would be a bit protective and help to take the place of his father. Uncle Bert didn't seem to offer much in that line.

Scott led the way through the crowd to the Wimpy Bar. He's quite fat, thought Rosemary. Not *really* fat, but *quite* fat. Scott was a nice name. Yeah, she liked him. She could talk to him. And he'd been super about that dog; she was looking forward to the burial ceremony that evening. She decided to pick a few flowers from her aunt's garden to put on the grave. She wondered whose pet the dog had been and how it had come to be in that old car. Funny, if she hadn't suggested looking in there for a wrench no one would ever have known. It was odd the way one thing led to another . . .

They sat down in a corner of the bar and when their tea and cakes arrived Scott looked at her with that friendly smile that had first made her stop and talk to him. "Tell me about your parents," he said. "How did the accident happen?"

Chapter 4

"And you understand what you've sworn?" said Hal. "You've sworn you won't *ever* tell *anyone* about our deal. You've sworn on your own blood and that's final for all your life."

Leo nodded. He was bandaging up his hand again with Hal's handkerchief, and a fresh red stain was soaking through the dirty white cotton.

"We'll do the handbag job first," Hal went on, "because that'll be an easy one for you to start with." He picked up a stone and got to his feet, aiming it at the seagull which still stood dreaming on the rock. The stone fell short but the gull flew hastily away, skimming the beach and landing on a distant breakwater.

"Could you just tell me the plan again," said Leo. "Some of it was a bit hard to follow."

"You'd better not mess it up, that's all," said Hal. "I've told you what I'll do if you muck things up, haven't I?"

Leo's heart thumped. It wasn't a threat against Leo himself, but against Rosemary, and the implications were too horrifying to think about. Leo had mentioned his sister to Hal the first time they met, when he told him about the death of his parents.

"*Listen*, then," growled Hal, "and I'll go through it again. You've got to listen to every-thing I say — and *do* everything I say."

"Yeah. O.K." Leo was worried about this handbag job. He was wishing in many ways that he'd never agreed to be Hal's business partner. Still, it was a terrific adventure and it meant he'd have some spending money. If his aunt wasn't going to give him his allow-ance he'd have to get some bread from *some-where*.

"Listen then! We meet at ten o'clock to-morrow morning outside the Plaza." The Plaza was a big white hotel at the posh end of the Promenade. "We go on the beach there because that's where the rich people are. We find some woman on her own with a handbag beside her — not holding it or looking at it. I ask her the time and while she's busy with me you whip the bag —"

"Very cool and quiet, like you said," broke in Leo, glad to show he had taken in some of the previous run-through.

"Right. So no one gets suspicious. Remember what I said — pick it up as if it was your mother's bag she'd asked you to fetch for her."

"Then I go off and hide it in a waste bin — "

"Not just any waste bin, you nit. The one we've decided on beforehand."

"Yeah — I know. But what if someone sees me?"

"You've got to be so cool that nobody'll think anything of it. Remember you're going to have a newspaper to wrap round the bag. Don't be such a baby."

Leo's hand was beginning to hurt intensely, but he knew he must concentrate. "What do I do then?" he said, biting his lips in an effort to look tough.

"Nothing else. Go home. But what am *I* doing all this time? Let's see if you've got that clear."

"As soon as I'm out of sight you tell the woman you thought you saw someone — a *girl* — run off with a handbag — and was it hers."

"*Then* what do I do — when she sees it's missing?"

"You — you — " Leo broke off. He'd forgotten the next step of the plan.

"*Then what?*" Hal stood over him. He took the knife out of his pocket, twisting it so that it caught the sun and flashed in Leo's eyes.

Leo struggled to remember. At last it came. "I know!" he gasped. "You tell the woman to stay where she is and you'll try and get it back."

Hal put the knife back in his inside pocket. "That's right. I tell her I saw where the girl went and I race off like lightning, get the bag out of the bin and — "

"And she gives you a reward," said Leo, grinning.

"Can't miss. I tell her I found the bag on the beach — the girl must have dropped it."

Leo let out a sigh. "So it won't be stealing, will it? Seeing that the woman gets it back?"

"Course not. We aren't stealing anything — I told you. I'm not going to risk any more trouble with the police." Hal had been cautioned the previous year when he pinched a bicycle.

Leo nodded. "And next day you give me my share of the reward. Ten percent."

"That's right."

"How do I know how much she gave you? I won't be there, will I?"

"What do you mean by that?" snapped

Hal. "You can't trust me?" His eyes were hard and bright as he stared down at Leo, his hands on his hips.

Leo stood up in order to feel less vulnerable but Hal still looked huge and sinister in his black leather jacket, with his blond hair blowing bright in the late sun.

Leo was silent, and at last Hal turned away, kicking a plastic bottle which had rolled to his feet in the scum of a wave. "You'll get your ten percent," he said. "I'll play straight with you if you do the same with me. But get this, Titch — "

"Don't call me that," said Leo.

"I'll call you what I want to. Get this, Titch — if you don't play straight I wouldn't like to be that sister of yours. I sure wouldn't like — "

"Hal — you mustn't hurt her — you mustn't ever — "

"Then don't you tell a soul about our deal."

"I *won't* — I *promise* — "

"Cos if you do, I'll — what's her name?"

"Rosemary. Oh, Hal, *please* — " He put out his hand with its bloody bandage to touch Hal's sleeve, and at that moment a soft voice broke in behind him. "You look upset, love. Anything the matter?"

Leo swung round to see a woman with wild gray hair and a red dress descending the steps from the road. When she reached him she stooped to look anxiously into his face. "Is there any trouble?" she asked.

Leo shook his head and kept his hand behind his back to hide the bandage. "N-no. No, thanks."

"You sounded so upset."

"I was just talking to my — my mate." He looked for Hal, frowning into the sun, but there was no sign of him; he had vanished like a ghost. If Leo hadn't seen the footprints in the sand, leading to a ladder in the sea wall nearby, he could almost have thought he had dreamed the whole painful encounter.

"So you're sure you're all right?" The woman smiled. It was a comforting smile that puffed out her wrinkled cheeks into shiny red balloons. Leo saw that she was carrying an old sack over her shoulder. The smile persisted, friendly and encouraging. "Where's your mate gone to?" she said.

Leo shrugged. "Dunno — home I 'spect. Home to his tea."

"And are you going home to your tea now?"

"Yeah. 'Spect so." Home, he thought. Aunt Kay's wasn't home; he didn't have a home any more . . .

The woman sauntered away along the rubbish-strewn beach. "I'm hunting for firewood," she called back to him. "Bits of old wood I can dry out and burn in the winter."

It it hadn't been for his cut hand Leo would have offered to help. As it was, he went slowly up the steps, noting with relief that his hand had stopped bleeding.

As he climbed, he caught sight of his old glob of bubble-gum stuck to the handrail. He paused with a grunt of pleasure to peel it off and put it in his mouth. There was still a bit of flavor left and it comforted him to blow it out and suck it in as he walked back to his aunt's house. It *is* my home really, he thought. Wherever Rosemary is, that's my home. But he wished he didn't feel so nervy about the next morning. Ten o'clock at the Plaza. Whatever happened he musn't make a mistake.

Chapter 5

"You don't *have* to tell me, if it upsets you," said Scott, taking a gulp of tea followed quickly by a bite of fruit tart. "It's not long ago, is it? April, did you say? Only four months."

Rosemary glanced round the Wimpy Bar. There was no one near enough to overhear their conversation. Four soldiers were talking together at the next table lost in a mist of smoke. A woman by the window was trying to pacify a crying child, and at the counter two waitresses were clattering dishes. Rosemary turned back to Scott. "I think I'd feel better if I told you," she said.

Scott was one of those people who look steadily into your face while you're talking, and his eyes were so big and dark and watch-ful that at first Rosemary felt shy. But not for long. It was a great relief to pour out the story of the air crash and how the news had reached her.

"They were on their way back from Ma-jorca," she told him. "Mum didn't want to go, but she'd had bronchitis all winter and Dad thought she needed a holiday in the sun. She really wanted to go somewhere in England so Leo and I could be there too. Anyway, Dad talked her into Majorca and —"

"Was it really because he wanted to go himself?" suggested Scott.

Rosemary hesitated, then nodded. She knew this was true, and there was something about Scott's great shining eyes that com-pelled her to be honest with him. "He was crazy about travel. He worked in a factory — engineering — but he'd really have loved to spend his life on the move — he often said so."

"But your mother wouldn't have liked that?"

"No — she was a home-lover. Like me, really."

Scott gave her an affectionate little smile. "Go on."

"Well, they left Leo and me with Aunt Kay and Uncle Bert — here where we're living now — and went off to Majorca on this package tour. It was awful for us because my aunt's terribly bossy and my uncle just goes to his office and hardly talks at all. He spends his spare time in the attic with a lot of old musical instruments — really peculiar." She took a sip of tea. "Mum and Dad were due back on the Saturday night — they were driving to Brinely from London Airport. That morning Aunt Kay cooked a chicken. I can remember the smell — it was there in the house all day. She was doing a cold supper so it woudn't matter if the plane was late — " She broke off; her voice had started to tremble but she was determined not to cry.

Scott said, "It's those little everyday things that are so upsetting, isn't it? My dad sent his watch away to be repaired and it came back the day after he died. This is the watch, actually." He held out his plump brown arm and Rosemary looked at the big silver watch with its worn leather strap.

She nodded sympathetically. "I've got my mother's jewelry to come — but not till I'm eighteen. That's three years to go."

"I'm eighteen today, as a matter of fact," said Scott.

"Many happy returns! What does it feel like?"

"Great. Can't quite believe it."

"Have this fruit pie of mine to celebrate. I don't really want it."

29

He grinned and began to eat the pie.

She went on, "That afternoon — the day they were due back — I was listening to the radio in my bedroom — keeping out of my aunt's way, as usual. It was a pop program and they have these news headlines every hour — you know. I don't usually listen much to the news but they said an airliner had crashed on takeoff in Majorca and there were no survivors. I *knew* it was their plane — I just *knew* it was — "

"Oh, God!" said Scott. "Hearing it like that, too."

"Yes, but the thing is, I didn't *tell* anybody! I didn't tell my aunt or uncle. Or Leo. I just kept quiet. I don't understand how I could have — but that's what happened. I just switched off the radio and said nothing. Later they were all talking about Mum and Dad coming back, and about the presents they'd bring us and all that — but I *still* didn't say a word."

"I can understand."

"But it frightens me, Scott. How could I have kept it to myself like that?"

"It was too awful to put into words — you just had to keep it locked up inside you. Some people would have shouted it all over the house, but I'm sure what you did was quite normal for *your* kind of person. We're all different."

"I get worried sometimes — thinking I'm not normal."

"What *is* normal? Nobody's normal. Just be *you*, and I'm sure you'll be all right."

She smiled at him shakily. He made her feel happier, easier, as if her worries were needless. "Anyway, I'll just tell you the rest. I was sick soon after I'd heard. They said it must be excitement at the thought of seeing Mum and Dad again."

"How *did* they find out?"

"From the telly — they saw the news and it said the passengers were all British holiday-makers. My aunt phoned the airport and got the flight number — and of course that was it. They just never came back." She didn't want to tell him about the funeral, or return-ing to their home in London to sort out her belongings. Or about the headaches she'd started getting . . .

Scott reached out his hand across the table and touched her arm. His brown eyes were soft with sympathy.

Rosemary said, "Just one more thing to tell you. All my aunt could say was 'It's Robert's fault — ' She blames my father for Mum getting killed."

"But he got killed too!"

"That doesn't make any difference to Aunt Kay. It's still his fault. She didn't want my mother to marry him in the first place. Mum

31

told me so. He was wild and untidy — not her sort at all. But Mum adored him. They were terribly happy —" She had to stop, quite unexpectedly, because her lips were quivering.

"It doesn't matter if you cry," said Scott. "Tell me."

"Aunt Kay says Mum would be alive today if it hadn't been for my father —"

"You mean she says that to *you*?"

"Not to me — to my uncle. But in *front* of me. In front of Leo, too — and he's only eleven."

"Isn't there anywhere else you could live except with them?"

"No — I've a granny in Scotland but she's too old to have us."

"So you've got to grin and bear it? Oh, well, I expect that's what you'll do. D'you want any more tea?"

She shook her head and got up. "I'd better go home and see if Leo's back. He's going to catch it from my aunt because he wouldn't go to Sunday School today. She's stopping his pocket money."

Scott groaned. "What a woman! That's enough to put him off religion for life."

"Losing our parents has put him off already — that's why he won't go! Last week he came home crying, poor kid. My aunt's got no idea how to handle him."

"Sounds as if she needs a psychology course! He's lucky to have you, anyway."

Scott paid the bill and they went out. Rosemary couldn't offer to pay her share because she'd come out without her shoulder bag. Next time she'd pay; somehow she was sure there would be a next time.

They stood in the sunny street and arranged to meet at the car dump later for the burial.

"Bye for now," she said. "I'll bring some flowers for the grave — or is that silly?"

"No — Course not. See you." Then he was gone, ambling away into the crowd. He had a rather slouchy way of walking, looking at the ground, but because she liked him so much, Rosemary found this endearing.

She headed for home, wondering if Leo would be there. She hoped he'd enjoyed himself with his new friend.

Chapter 6

"*Please* let me come with you," said Leo. "I've never seen a dead dog."

Rosemary burst out laughing. "You grizzly little horror!"

Leo had intercepted her on her way to the garden gate. She was wearing a long brown skirt and a lacy blouse and her hair was held back in a barrette. She looked older than usual, and she was carrying a bunch of roses. She must have picked them from the front garden.

"Can I come?" He wanted to be with her, quite apart from the appeal of the burial; the stress of the afternoon with Hal had upset him. Besides, it might mean he could stay up longer; he hated going to bed on these long summer evenings. "Please!" he implored.

She looked down at him and her big gray eyes had that loving shine that told him she might agree. He was reminded of his mother when she looked at him like that. For a few moments her small face was serious and undecided, and then she smiled. The smile, too, was like his mother's had been — sudden and wonderfully bright. "All right," she said. "But don't tell *them* about it. They'd only fuss." "Them" always meant Aunt Kay and Uncle Bert, who were now safely involved with a favorite television program.

Leo and Rosemary set off for the car dump and after a while she asked him if he'd found Hal that afternoon.

"No. He wasn't there."

"What did you do, then?"

"Just played in The Winner."

"What? With no money to spend?"

"I just watched people." Leo was getting nervy.

"And then you played on the beach?"

"*No.* I never went *near* the beach." If only she wouldn't pry so much; she was like a grown-up sometimes.

"But you told Aunt Kay you cut your hand on a piece of glass on the beach?"

Leo's heart was thudding. "I told *her* that — but it wasn't true. I cut it on my penknife."

"Why couldn't you have said so?" asked Rosemary. By now they were near the car dump.

"I thought she'd be cross — I thought she might take my knife away from me."

Rosemary sighed. "Yeah — I suppose she might have. Still, you can always tell *me* the truth, pet. Then I can help you, can't I?"

Leo nodded but he knew he couldn't. He had sworn to tell no one about his business deal with Hal and he wished with all his heart that it wasn't so.

Scott had already arrived and was digging energetically with a big spade, throwing up great lumps of earth and grass. He had chosen a spot behind the old blue car.

"Hi!" said Rosemary. "This is my brother Leo."

Scott smiled and Leo liked his placid, rosy face. He was big and easy and comfortable-looking and his smile was friendly and not in the least condescending. Being small for his age, Leo found that older boys could be very off-hand. Or menacing, like Hal.

"I can dig," said Leo.

"O.K. — have a go. I could do with a rest."

Scott handed Leo the spade and he grasped the warm handle but as soon as he started to dig, his palm began to hurt. Every time he lifted a spadeful of earth it hurt him more, but he was determined not to say anything, having made the offer.

Rosemary was holding out the roses to show Scott and he was sniffing at them and nodding at her as if it was quite reasonable to put flowers on a dog's grave. Leo thought it was silly.

After a while Scott said to Leo, "That's great — I'll finish it off now," and thankfully Leo handed over the spade.

When the grave was completed Scott removed the lid of the trunk and Leo forgot his throbbing hand in the fascination of seeing the dead terrier. He was reminded of his kitten which had died of cat flu and had lain so stiff and lusterless, its blank eyes crawling with flies. This dog, also massed with flies, had been dead much longer and was less pitiful, having so little resemblance to its living self. It was more like a battered old doormat. Leo watched with interest but without distress as Scott lifted it with the spade and slid it gently into the grave.

"Ought we to say a prayer for it?" said Rosemary, looking doubtfully at Scott.

Leo thought this was another silly idea and he was just going to say so when he saw a moving shadow beside him on the grass. He looked round to see a policeman approaching.

"What's all this, then?" The policeman was

thin and white-faced, as if he had just been ill. He had a fiery red pimple on his chin.

"Just burying a dog," replied Scott cheerfully. "Found it in the trunk of this old car."

The policeman rummaged in his pocket and brought out a notebook and pencil.

"Let's have your name," he said gruffly.

"Do I — I mean — is it against the law to — ?"

"Your name, please?"

"Scott Fleming."

"Address?"

"Nineteen, Marine Street. I thought I was doing a service, actually — getting it buried."

The policeman said nothing. He was writing in his notebook. When he had finished he turned to inspect Rosemary and Leo.

Scott said, "They've got nothing to do with it. They're just — "

"*I* have," said Rosemary. "I've got some flowers to put on the grave." She thrust them under the policeman's nose and he took a step backwards.

"And I helped to dig it," put in Leo defiantly. He had been taught by his parents to look on policemen as friends and he was affronted by the hostility of this one.

"Who's dog is it?" said the policeman.

Scott explained the events of the afternoon while the policeman scratched at the spot on his chin, making it redder than ever.

"How did you know the dog was in the trunk?"

Scott hesitated. He had said nothing about the side-mirror.

"We smelled it," said Rosemary quickly. "We thought is might spread disease if it was left, so Scott decided to bring a spade and bury it."

The policeman sighed and grunted and returned his notebook and pencil to his pocket.

"Is it all right then?" said Leo.

The policeman ignored him and addressed himself to Scott. "Fill that hole in quickly and clear off," he said. "This land belongs to the Council. You can't start digging holes whenever it takes your fancy."

He walked away briskly without looking back and when he was out of earshot Rosemary burst out, "How rotten! He should have *thanked* you — doing a good turn like that. He's got no right to *be* a policeman!"

"Come on," said Scott, "let's get on with it. I've brought a wrench to get that mirror but I don't feel like doing it now." He covered the dog with earth and flattened the surface of the grave with the back of the spade.

Rosemary laid the flowers on top.

"They'll die," said Leo.

"Come on," said Scott. "Let's get out of

here." There was a grim set to his mouth.

"I want to say a prayer for it," said Rosemary.

"Hurry up then," said Scott irritably. "I'm going on."

"I *can't* hurry — I don't know what to *say*."

Leo said, "*Dogs* don't need *prayers!*"

Scott was already heading for the road and Rosemary stared mutely at the grave for a moment, then started to run after him. Leo caught them up and tagged on behind.

"What's up with you, Scott?" said Rosemary. "Are you mad that you couldn't get your mirror?"

"Course not — I'm not bothered by that."

"What then?"

"I don't want my name and address in a policeman's notebook, that's what!"

"You haven't done anything wrong."

"He thinks I have."

"Not really. It won't come to anything."

Scott was silent and Leo felt sorry for him as he walked behind them, kicking a stone along.

Rosemary turned around and called out to him, "Leo — you go off home now — it's your bedtime."

"No — I want to stay with you and Scott."

"You can't. We're going for a drink. It's Scott's birthday."

"Can't I come?"

"Course not — were going to a *pub*, silly."

"You can't — you're not allowed."

"Well, I'm going anyway. Go on home, Leo. And not a word to *them*." She turned to Scott, and Leo heard her say in an undertone, "He won't tell — you can trust him with anything."

This made him glow with such sudden joy that he went racing off home without another word. When he'd got enough money he'd buy Rosemary a necklace or something. He was suddenly eager for the next morning and the handbag job. He wished Hal was a bit more like Scott. He really liked Scott.

Chapter 7

Uncle Bert was in the front room when Rosemary arrived home that Sunday night. He was sitting in an easy chair reading one of his musical magazines but she had seen him looking out of the window when she said good-night to Scott at the front gate. Scott hadn't kissed her but he had taken her hand and held it for a long time while they arranged their next meeting. Sharon, the girl next door, had been peeping, too. She was a big clumsy girl with a discontented mouth and she seemed to spend half her time nosing into other people's affairs.

"Hello, uncle," said Rosemary. "Did Leo get to bed O.K.?"

"Oh, yes. No trouble. He's a good little lad." There was a pause and Bert shut the magazine and put it on the table beside him. "Who was the boyfriend?" he asked.

"He's a student — sociology."

Uncle Bert was always kind and pleasant to Rosemary and Leo when Aunt Kay wasn't there. She had continually upbraided him for "spoiling" his niece and nephew and now he only made real contact when Kay was out.

"Have you known him long?" Bert was a thin, sad-faced little man with lank gray hair and nervous twitchy movements. Rosemary felt sorry for him. There seemed to be no affection between him and his wife — no loving glances, no laughs and cuddles and secrets. They only spoke of essentials (*"Have you paid the gas bill, Bert?"* or *"Kay, where's my green pullover?"*) and they hardly ever smiled except when they were watching a comedy show on television.

"Known him long?" repeated Bert.

"No — only today." Rosemary undid her barrette and shook out her hair. "Why?"

Uncle Bert shifted uncomfortably in his chair. He picked up the magazine and put it down again, coughed, and looked at his fingernails. Then he said, "I don't want to upset you, dear — but I — well, I wonder if — you've been told — "

"It's all right, uncle," said Rosemary cheerfully. "I'm quite well-informed about sex, if that's what you mean. Mummy told me years ago."

Bert glanced at her with a little smile and looked relieved. "Well, that's fine. You're an attractive girl and you look more than fifteen, you know. More like seventeen. You really must be careful — very careful indeed. I had to mention it because your aunt — well, she'd find it difficult to say anything — you know what I mean?"

Rosemary knew. Aunt Kay was very prudish; it was clear from her reactions to sexy films or plays on television. Sometimes she got up and went out of the room and sometimes she even switched off the set.

"Don't worry, uncle," said Rosemary. "I can take care of myself." She thought it was time to change the subject. "Has Aunt Kay gone out?"

"Yes — gone to see a friend who's sick. A woman at the shop." The gown shop where Kay worked was an exclusive little place at the smart end of Brinely. It usually had one simple dress in the window with no price on it. Kay got soiled garments or old stock at big reductions and always managed to look well dressed.

Suddenly Rosemary wanted to make a friend of her uncle. Now was the time, while Kay was out and Leo asleep. "Uncle Bert," she said. "Would you do something for me?"

His sad eyes brightened as he looked up at her. "Of course I will. What is it, dear?"

"Will you show me all your violins and trumpets and things in the attic?"

He was on his feet in an instant, his face alive with pleasure and eagerness. "I'd be delighted," he cried. "*Delighted.* Come along. It's a bit dusty but you won't mind that, will you? I've just got a new addition to my collection — a beautiful lute — really beautiful. Just wait till you see it!" He was on his way up the red stairs, stumbling in his haste, chattering on about his lute, glancing back to make sure that Rosemary was following.

He hurried up the second flight — a bare creaking staircase leading to the attic — and switched on the light. The room was lit by a single electric bulb hanging from the low ceiling. Rosemary had been up there several times but never after dark and never with her uncle.

She sat on an old cabin trunk and gazed around at the array of musical instruments. They filled the room, lying on boxes and suitcases and piles of magazines. There were guitars and mandolins, a cello gaping open with a split side, its front as shiny as a newly peeled chestnut. By the window hung a trumpet, black with age, and on the floor stood a great harp, greenish-gold in the murky light, its strings casting stripes of shadow on the wall. On a broken chair was a kettle drum and under the chair a dusty violin.

"Can you play any of them?" asked Rosemary kindly, but she knew the answer; she had listened on the stairs when he was practicing, and the noise was enough to start up one of her headaches.

"Not really — but I'm trying. One day, perhaps — if I could afford to have lessons." He was carefully unwrapping a big brown paper parcel and soon he was holding out to her his latest acquisition.

"There!" he murmured. "Isn't she a beauty?"

Rosemary took the lute from him and held it on her lap. She loved the simple shape of it — it reminded her of a boat — and the facets of wood were a pale golden brown, the color of the beer she had drunk in the pub with Scott. "It's lovely," she said.

"It's worth quite a bit — I'm paying for it by installments. But don't tell your aunt, will you? I *had* to have it — you can see that, can't you?" He glanced at her anxiously.

She nodded, touching the round design under the strings and marveling at the intricate carving. She was thinking that a pattern of lutes would make a beautiful wallpaper for a music room.

"That's called the rose," Bert told her.

"It's carved to look like interwoven basket-work."

Rosemary examined it with new respect. "Why do you collect all these instruments?" she asked, handing back the lute. "Are you going to do them up and sell them?"

"Oh, *no*. I'd never do that. Couldn't bear to part with a single one." He was wrapping the lute in its paper again. "I'm too fond of them, you see. Much too fond of them."

Rosemary was just about to ask if she could help him to tidy things up when she held her breath, hearing the sound of some-one crying. It was a stifled sobbing that grew more piteous every moment.

"It's Leo!" she gasped. "I must go to him."

"Shall I come with you?"

"No — no thanks." She raced down the stairs to her brother's room and was soon on her knees beside his bed.

"Leo — what is it? What's the matter?" The light from the landing fell across his pil-low and she saw that his mouth was twisted with misery, his face streaked with a mixture of dirt and tears.

"I don't — want to —" he whimpered.

She stroked his hand, seeing the dried blood around the plaster on his palm. "Don't want to what, pet? What don't you want?"

"I — don't *want* to —" He began to cry again.

"Tell me. Tell me, Leo?"

"No — I can't —"

"Course you can. Come on, *tell* me."

He shook his head, burying his face in the pillow.

She stayed beside him, anxious as a mother, and soon he lay quiet, breathing heavily.

"Are you asleep?" she whispered.

There was no reply and she tip-toed out of the room. He must have had a bad dream, she thought. Poor little scrap, maybe his hand had been hurting him.

Soon she was lying in her own bed, drowsily thinking through the events of the day, remembering her long, intimate conversations with Scott. It was hard to believe that yesterday she had not even known he existed.

Chapter 8

"So you didn't chicken out?" said Hal. His
hair was neatly combed and he was wearing
a spotless yellow shirt and smart green trous-
ers. He was obviously dressed for the part he
was to play, the part of a responsible, helpful
young citizen. Leo had on the same blue T-
shirt and jeans he'd worn the day before.
There were bloodstains on his shirt and he
didn't want to change it; he was proud of
that blood.

"Course I didn't chicken out," he said
scornfully, feeling strong with morning con-
fidence. "Come on, let's get going." He turned
his back on the great white frontage of the
Plaza Hotel and started off in the direction
of the beach.

A well-mown grassy slope, bordered with red geraniums, lay between the Promenade and the sea. At intervals, wide steps of glittery pink stone led down to the beach. Already the sky was a shimmering blue. The sands were filling up with holiday-makers lounging in deck-chairs, walking at the water's edge, splashing in the gentle waves. Some were playing ball games, and Leo couldn't help wishing he was here to play cricket with Rosemary instead of being committed to the handbag job. Still, he needed the money very badly; he hadn't even enough for a pack of bubble-gum.

"Leo — come *back*!" Hal's voice was sharp, and Leo turned and retraced his steps.

"What's up?" he said.

"I just want to get it clear about the money. We'll meet here tomorrow — same time — and I'll give you ten percent of whatever I get. If she gives me a pound you get 10p. Five pounds and you get 50p. Right?"

Leo looked Hal straight in the eye. For an instant he hesitated and then he said, "No. I don't think it's enough. I take the risks, don't I? It's *me* that gets clobbered if we're caught."

"Who's idea was it?" Hal was scowling.

"Yours, but — "

"Who swore to do *everything* I said?"

Leo was silent but he stood his ground,

hoping for a concession. Passersby were buffeting against them as they stood at the edge of the pavement but Leo was unaware of them, waiting eagerly for Hal's next words.

"Tell you what, Titch. If this job goes all right I'll put you up a bit for the next one. O.K.?"

Leo nodded and set off down the broad pink steps to the beach.

"Haven't you forgotten something?" said Hal.

Leo swung around nervously. "What?"

"The litter bin, you nit. We've got to choose the *bin*."

"I hadn't forgotten," said Leo untruthfully. "That one there!" The bin was a large metal one attached to a railing. It was painted green and had *Litter Please* marked on the side.

"That's good, being next to a telephone box," said Hal. "We can't mistake it. You're framing well. Take note of some other things around — that bus stop — the zebra crossing, the Plaza across the road. You've got to *notice* things —"

"O.K. — let's get going," said Leo, and now Hal followed him as he raced down onto the sands.

They sauntered together among the holiday-makers, looking carefully for unattended handbags. Most of the women had their bags on their laps or close beside them, but after a while Leo spotted a woman in a red sunhat who was kneeling down beside a small boy. She was making sand-pies for him, tipping them out of a little bucket. The child was standing beside her but he had lost interest and was sucking a stick of rock candy and gazing up at a kite which fluttered overhead. The woman's handbag, a shiny brown one with a gilt clasp, was lying a few feet away, together with a towel and a pair of sunglasses.

"Hal — look!" Leo touched Hal's arm and pointed to the bag.

"Don't *point*, you fool!" muttered Hal. Leo saw him studying the situation — the woman's diligent pie-making, the little boy engrossed in the kite, the handbag easily accessible behind them.

"Get it now," whispered Hal. "Very casual, remember. Go on — *now!*"

"What about your asking her the time?" Leo's legs were beginning to shake.

"There's no *need*. Go *on!*"

Leo went boldly forward and picked up the bag by its short leather strap. It was heavier than it looked and as he strode away he felt as if everyone on the beach was watching him. It wasn't until he was on his way up the steps to the road that he realized he had no newspaper to wrap it in. They had both forgotten this vital bit of preparation.

Leo felt he must look ridiculous as well as suspicious — a boy of eleven with a lady's handbag! He clutched it under his arm and began to run, racing towards the telephone box as fast as he could go. He had to get it into the bin quickly, quickly, before anyone saw him . . .

"Hello, Leo! Where are *you* off to?"

Leo stopped as if he'd been shot, trying to cover the bag with his hand, and found himself looking into the grinning, bespectacled face of Dicky Robertson, a boy in his form at school. "N — nowhere — " he stuttered.

"I've been shopping for my mum," Dicky said, holding up a string bag full of groceries. "Can you come and look in the toy shops?" Dicky shared Leo's passion for model racing cars and they had spent some good times together looking in shop windows.

"Can't stop — sorry — got to rush — " Leo dived into the crowd and was obliged to hurry away from the litter bin in order to conceal himself from Dicky.

At the bus stop a line of people was waiting, and Leo joined the end of it, holding the handbag against his chest, trembling from head to foot. Dicky seemed to have vanished and when a bus drew up and the people got in, leaving Leo in isolation, he walked back to the litter bin, staring straight in front of him, his chest so tight with strain that he could hardly breathe.

With one terrified lunge, he stuffed the bag into the bin on top of a crumple of greasy paper. No one seemed to be taking any notice, and he launched himself onto the zebra crossing. He'd done it — *done* it! The tension in his chest was gone and a little smile was tugging at the corners of his mouth. He was safe, he'd completed his mission; Hal would be pleased with him.

Then suddenly, on the opposite pavement, he was face to face with Dicky Robertson again, still grinning, his glasses flashing in the sun.

"What was the hurry?" said Dicky.

"What do *you* think? Couldn't wait."

"Shall we go and look at the shops?"

"If you like."

"Just a sec, then," said Dicky. "I want to fish out that bag you put in the rubbish bin. My mum collects things like that for jumble sales. It looked quite good — "

"*No!*" Leo's voice came out so loudly a man stopped to stare at him. "No — it wasn't any good — all rotten — with a big hole in it — no good to anybody. Honest." His chest was tight again.

Dicky looked surprised and disappointed. "Are you sure? I thought it looked quite new. Where did you find it?"

"It was just — kicking about the street. I thought there might be something in it but it was empty so I threw it away. Come on, let's go to Hunter's." Hunter's was the biggest toy shop in Brinely.

Leo told himself that there was nothing to worry about; Dicky wasn't bright enough to make anything of it. He glanced back at the litter bin and as he did so he caught sight of Hal, his yellow shirt and blond hair unmistakable. He was rummaging in the bin and Leo saw him pull out the handbag and go marching away towards the beach with it, head held high, smoking a cigarette. He's so *brave*, thought Leo . . .

Dicky was walking ahead, trailing his mother's string bag on the ground; he couldn't have seen Hal. So it was all right! Provided the woman came up with a decent reward, the job was a complete success. Leo hoped to goodness that Hal would play straight and tell him the truth about it. Still, there was no way of finding out so he'd just have to trust him. Golly, it was exciting. He wondered what his next assignment would be; he hoped it was something that would bring in a really big reward . . .

He caught Dicky up and put his hand on his shoulder. "You know that racing car I wanted?" he said. "That green one in Hunter's?"

Dicky nodded. "Yeah — I know — Formula One. Big scale model."

"Well, I think I'll be getting it quite soon. *Think* I will, anyway."

"Lucky devil!" said Dicky.

Leo supposed he was lucky, but somehow the racing car had lost a lot of its appeal, and he wasn't quite sure why.

Chapter 9

"Rosemary — you're not to go out till you've washed up the breakfast things and dusted the living room." It was Monday morning, three weeks later. Aunt Kay stood in the kitchen doorway ready to leave for work. Uncle Bert had gone an hour earlier and Leo was in his room.

Rosemary grunted. Her aunt was wearing a shiny green suit with a gilt spider brooch in the lapel. Rosemary hated spiders and couldn't understand how anybody could wear one as an ornament.

"What are you going to do today? Going out with the boyfriend?"

At least she's been nice about Scott, thought Rosemary; it must be because her aunt wanted her married and off her hands as soon as possible.

"No — he's got a holiday job. Porter at the railway station."

"Seeing him tonight?"

"Not till nine — at the Disco. He's got a lecture."

"He studies hard — I'll say that for him. Well, I must go or I'll be late. Don't forget the dusting."

Studies hard! thought Rosemary. He studies *too* jolly hard. She began the washing up, dabbing irritably at a greasy plate. In three weeks her friendship with Scott had grown into a serious romance but she was more and more frustrated by his obsession with work. A big exam was looming up and he was preparing a thesis on prison reform. Work came before the Disco, before swimming and picnics, before the cinema. She had to face the fact that sometimes work came before Rosemary! When they were apart she counted the hours till their next meeting and every time she saw him she felt more certain that she would love him forever. Yet he had never said he loved her and she was sick with worry in case he never would.

She was cleaning the greasy sink when the kitchen door burst open and Leo appeared. He was holding something behind his back.

"What's that you've got?" snapped Rosemary. Her resentment against Scott was sometimes vented on Leo.

"It's for you," he said gruffly. "It's a present." He held out a brown paper bag.

Rosemary dried her hands on the tea towel. "But it isn't my birthday or anything — " What had come over him? They'd hardly seen each other of late, except for meals.

"Doesn't matter. Go on — open it."

She took it gingerly. Leo's presents were always unpredictable. It might be anything from a bar of chocolate to a tortoise.

"Whatever can it be?" She felt at the bag, delaying the moment for his sake, watching the glow of expectancy on his round, freckled face.

"Go on — open it!"

Inside the bag was a long string of bright blue beads. It was only a plastic necklace but to Rosemary it was like a rope of sapphires. "Oh Leo — it's beautiful!" She hugged him awkwardly and he wriggled away, watching her with bashful pleasure as she put the beads around her neck. She wondered how he got the money. He still refused to go to Sunday School and as far as Rosemary knew, her aunt had continued to punish him by withholding his allowance. "Leo, I thought you were broke. Has Aunt Kay given you some money after all?"

"No, she hasn't. But I've got plenty, don't

you worry. I don't need *her* to give me any."

"But how did you get it?"

His face was suddenly crimson and she was anxious, remembering how strange and shifty he had been of late. Ever since he began to go out with Hal he had been withdrawn and uncommunicative, rushing to his room when he came in, unwilling to talk about his activities.

"Leo," she persisted. "Tell me how you got the money."

"I *earned* it."

"What doing?"

"All sorts of things. Odd jobs."

"What? Who for?"

"Don't *nag* me. I've forgotten."

"I'm not nagging — I just want to know."

"It's *my* money, and I —"

"Course it is — and I'm thrilled with my present — but you've been so odd lately — I've been worried about you. You're always out with Hal but you never *talk* about him, do you? You never tell me anything. Why don't you?"

Leo was kicking at a piece of torn linoleum on the floor. "I've got to go now," he muttered.

"To meet Hal?"

Leo nodded.

"Where are you meeting him?"

He was silent for a moment, then he said

in a low voice, "It's a secret."

"Why?"

"Oh, stop nagging me. I've got to *go* — "

She sighed. It was no use trying to press him now. "Thanks for the beads," she said. I'll wear them tonight at the Disco."

"With Scott?"

She nodded. "You like him, don't you?"

"Yeah. Are you going to marry him?"

"Leo — don't be so *silly*. I've only known him three weeks."

"I've seen you kissing and cuddling at the gate."

"What's wrong with that?"

"Nothing."

"All right, then. Go on with you."

He ran out of the back door and she took off the necklace, tenderly fingering it. Fancy him spending his money on her like that! But how did he get it? She'd been so wrapped up in dreams of Scott that she'd hardly paid any attention to Leo. And her aunt and uncle certainly hadn't. She had to see this Hal and find out. She had to see him *now* . . .

In a minute she was out in the street, just in time to catch a glimpse of Leo heading for the Promenade. Cautiously she followed him, keeping her distance but taking care that he didn't disappear from view. She felt excited. Hal was about her own age; she wondered what he would be like . . .

She stalked Leo through the town, feeling like a spy, and he made his way to an open market on the seafront. It was a noisy, colorful place, bustling with holiday crowds. There were stalls selling hot dogs, souvenirs, postcards, mussels, Brinely rock. It was behind the mussel stall that Leo met up with Hal. Rosemary hid behind a parked van so she could watch them without being seen.

Leo was soon in deep conversation with this tall fair boy in a black leather jacket. Rosemary liked the looks of him. His smooth hair shone like gold in the morning sun and his profile was clear and strong against the dark blue of the sea. She admired the way he stood so straight and self-assured, the poise of his handsome head, the nonchalant way he lit a cigarette, cupping the match in his hand as her father used to do.

Leo seemed to be protesting about something. He was shaking his head and Hal was frowning, arguing back. This went on for some time until Leo became less agitated, nodded his head and ran off into the crowd. Hal threw away his cigarette butt and set off briskly in the opposite direction, lighting up another.

Rosemary hesitated for an instant and then she raced after him. From time to time he was lost among the strolling holiday-makers but his bright hair was easy to spot and at last she caught him up.

"I say — just a sec," she gasped. "I want to talk to you. I'm Leo's sister."

Hal turned and she saw that his eyes were brilliantly blue. "Well, how about that?" he said, looking her up and down. "So you're the wonderful Rosemary! Very nice, too."

"I just want to ask about Leo — "

"What about him?" Hal's face stiffened.

"Well, I'm a bit worried — he's bought me some beads but he won't tell me how he got the money. Says he's been earning it — odd jobs and — "

"What's it to do with me?" Hal drew viciously on his cigarette and threw it away, half smoked.

"I don't know, but he wouldn't say where he was meeting you. Said it was a secret. That's why I followed him — to find out — and talk to you."

"You *followed* him?" Hal glared at her angrily. "You want to watch it, girl. Just you watch it, that's all!"

"What d'you mean?" She felt vaguely afraid of him, even there on the busy pavement.

"I mean what I say. *Watch* it!" He reached out and seized her by the wrist, holding it so tightly that she almost cried out.

"Let go of me — you're hurting!"

"Sorry," he said, relaxing his grip. "I don't know my own strength — I've been told that before." He smiled at her, a slow intimate smile that set her heart thumping. "Gorgeous girl you are, Rosemary."

"Shut up — I'm worried about Leo."

"He's all right. Boys like him don't want their sisters prying on them." Now he took her hand and held it very gently. "How about a date? I'd like to take you out." The expression in his eyes made her tingle with excitement and she really had no wish to refuse. If Scott heard she'd been around with an attractive boy like Hal, he might realize how much he valued her.

"All right," she said. "I don't mind."

"Have you seen that Paul Newman film at the Roxy?"

She shook her head. It was a film she wanted to see with Scott but he might never get around to taking her, with all his studying.

"Tonight, then?" said Hal.

"Can't make it tonight — I'm going to the Disco."

"Tomorrow?"

"All right."

"You really are a stunner, Rosemary." He gripped her shoulder for a moment, making her acutely aware of his male domination.

"I've got to go now," he told her. "See you at seven tomorrow."

Scott never makes me feel like this, she thought, as she watched him hurry away. Scott was loving and gentle and gave her a wonderful sense of happiness and peace, but with Hal her pulses raced with excitement. It was almost as if she was in danger, and yet somehow she couldn't help wanting more of it. When he had disappeared from view she stood by the sea wall and wondered what she would wear for the Roxy the following evening.

Chapter 10

When Leo went off to meet Hal after giving Rosemary the necklace, he felt a peculiar mixture of joy and fear. He was happy because he had bought his sister a present that delighted her, but he had obviously made her suspicious. Whatever he bought, it would be the same: she would wonder where he got the money . . .

There was something else that made him sick with anxiety as he hurried through the sunny streets: Hal was planning the biggest job ever — something that could bring in a huge reward, he said; "enough to make a fiver look like peanuts." Today was the day, and Leo was scared of what he might have to do.

During the past three weeks he had successfully managed more than a dozen jobs. He'd knocked down a candy stall so that Hal could set it up again; he'd stolen a cat from a garden so that Hal could "find" it and return it to the anguished old lady whose pet it was; he'd set fire to a pile of rubbish in someone's back yard so that Hal could put out the fire and inform the owner of the house. Hal had received a fiver for that and given Leo a pound. Leo's share for the other jobs had been only a few pence. Sometimes there was no real reward at all — or so Hal said. Every day Leo trusted him less, feared him more, and wished with all this heart that he had never become involved.

At first it had all been fun, exciting, gloriously dangerous; a way of getting kicks and earning enough money to buy bubble-gum and enjoy himself in The Winner. But now the early sense of fun and challenge was gone. Every day Leo became more sickened by these escapades and the trouble they caused to innocent people. Yet Hal became more menacing. "You don't want anything to happen to that sister of yours, do you?" he would say if Leo protested. And he would go on to describe Rosemary's fate if Leo broke his pledge. It seemed there was no way out . . .

And now he was facing "the biggest job yet" and his chest felt tight as he saw Hal waiting behind the mussel stall in the market place. He was sure his luck couldn't hold out much longer. Soon he'd get caught and he dared not think what would happen to him then.

Hal was smoking a cigarette, as usual. "Hello, Titch. What are you looking so sulky about?"

"I'm not," said Leo, biting his lip.

"Yes, you are. Now listen to me — I've got it all worked out —"

Hal lowered his voice but here there was really no need. The tourists flocked around them, buying from the stalls, intent on their own activities. Seagulls circled above, traffic rumbled by, the waves broke against the sea wall. The sun was hot on Leo's bare arms, burning his forehead.

"You'll have to be very careful," said Hal, "but you can't go wrong if you do as I say and —"

"What *is* it then?" said Leo impatiently. "What am I going to do?"

"You're going to steal a baby. You're —"

"I'm *not*," burst out Leo. "I'm bloody *not!*"

"Yes, you are!"

"No, I'm not!"

"And I say you are." Hal held his cigarette dangerously near Leo's arm. "The kid's in its carriage on the beach near the Plaza every morning with its mother. She lives in a big house up there — must be loaded. With

68

any luck we'll get something really big out of it."

"I don't want to do it, Hal." Leo's voice was husky with nerves. "Let's think of something else — *please!*"

"Shut up! I've done a lot of work on this — been on the beach every day — and we're damn well going through with it. Now listen to me: the woman goes swimming at about half past ten. She leaves the baby in the carriage down near the water while she goes into a bathing hut to change. The beach is crowded solid and nobody's going to notice you push the carriage away while she's in the hut."

Leo's heart was thumping so fiercely that he could hardly breathe. The idea of taking a woman's baby away from her appalled him, quite apart from the dangers of discovery. "But what if — ?"

"What if nothing," said Hal. "Pretend you're the kid's brother. Nobody's going to think anything unless you act suspicious."

"How old's the baby?"

"Few months, by the look of it. It's always been asleep when I've seen it."

"Suppose it wakes up and yells?"

"So what? Kids are yelling all over the place. Now *listen* while I tell you where to take it." Hal came closer and Leo could smell his smoky breath as he went on urgently, "There's an old boatshed next to the pier — hasn't been used for ages. Do you know it?"

Leo nodded miserably. It was about ten minutes' walk from the Plaza.

"There's a big fishing boat in there," said Hal. "Rotting away. If you push the carriage behind it nobody'll find it till I come and get it."

"But people'll see me and —"

"They won't think anything. Don't forget the kid won't have been missed — its mother'll still be in the bathing hut."

"What then?"

"Easy! You leave the pram in there and scram. I watch out for her coming out of the hut and do the usual. You know — tell her I saw a girl push the carriage away and think I saw where she went. Tell the woman to wait and —"

"Hal, I can't —"

"You mean you *won't*?"

"No, I —"

"Remember Rosemary! Is she pretty?"

Leo's heart lurched. "Yes — she is."

"Well, she won't be, will she? Not if —"

"All right," burst out Leo. "All right. Tell me again. Tell me *exactly*."

Hal repeated the directions, describing the plump woman, the low blue carriage with its small wheels and white sun canopy, the dark-haired baby. "Now get going," he concluded. "And I'll see you in The Winner tomorrow for the hand-out. Ought to be really something."

Leo ran off into the crowd without another word. He felt sick with dread but it seemed there was nothing to do but carry out Hal's orders. Please God, he thought, please make it all right! God was gradually becoming a power in his life again and as he made his way towards the beach he was praying with all his might that something would happen to deliver him from Hal.

On his way to the Plaza beach Leo looked in at the boatshed. The old fishing boat lay on its side, its gaping timbers encrusted with limpets and barnacles. Behind it was a dark corner, and there was an easy ramp leading up to it. Perhaps it wasn't going to be so difficult after all . . .

He hurried along towards the bathing huts. The sands were so crowded he was afraid he would never find the woman with the carriage. People lay on towels and in deck chairs. An old man slept under a newspaper sun-hat; two fat women in bikinis were rubbing each other with oil; people in the water splashed and shrieked. Trenches were dug. Beach balls bounced on the firm sand. The sun blazed. And Leo suddenly caught sight of the blue carriage with its white fringed canopy. It shone out for him on that crowded beach as if it was under a spotlight, and the woman lying on a towel beside it filled Leo with terror because he was going to do this appalling thing to her.

Slowly he approached. He had to examine the carriage, make sure he knew how to release the brake, assess the whole situation. The woman was lying on her side with her back to the sun. She wore a pink dress and was reading a book. Her face was plain but pleasant and Leo saw that she was smiling secretly as she read. He sauntered by, reminding himself that he looked quite ordinary and that no one could guess what was in his mind. The baby was asleep on its back — a pale-faced mite with black curly hair. It was dressed in a yellow blouse and shorts; a woolly rabbit lay beside its tiny bare feet.

Suddenly the woman sat up and gazed at the sea, wrinkling her eyes against the glare of it. She laid her open book on the towel, picked up her beach bag and scrambled awkwardly to her feet. She looked into the pram, adjusted the hood to keep the sun off the baby's face and headed for the beach huts without a backward glance.

Leo's stomach was cold with fear. He watched the woman go into one of the huts and close the door behind her. There was no window; she couldn't possibly see him.

Now was the time. No one was taking any notice of him. The baby slept. A little breeze turned the pages of the book on the towel. A big dog cantered by, spraying Leo with sand.

With a tremendous effort of will he took hold of the carriage handle. The ridged rubber was hot with the sun. He must do it now. He *must* . . . He was just about to kick off the brake when the baby opened its eyes and looked at him.

Instantly Leo let go of the handle. The baby's eyes were dark blue and brightly attentive. They were fixed on Leo's face with a calm watchful trust. Leo remembered that he must behave as if he was the baby's brother and he made a brave attempt to smile at it. Instantly the baby responded. Its doll-like face expanded into a sweet toothless grin and it began to kick its feet, rocking the pram and shaking the fringes of the canopy.

At that moment Leo knew that he could not take this baby away from its mother. It was as if a voice was speaking to him quite clearly: No, it said. No, No, *No* . . .

The baby was still kicking happily, staring blandly out of those calm, bright eyes. Then Leo turned and ran. He ran off the beach, along the Promenade, out of the town. He ran until he was breathless, making his way to a deserted gulley along the cliffs. He lay down in the sandy grass, feeling as helpless and frightened as a child of six. He wanted his mother, and the tears were very close. Suddenly a seagull alighted only a few yards away. It stood there, glossy and plump in the sun, quite unaware of his presence, and it looked so composed, so sure of its place in the universe, that he lay and watched it quietly for a while, his terrors abating. Then some hikers came by and it lifted away into the sparkling sky, free and unconcerned. But when the people had passed, the spell was broken; Leo buried his face in his arms and burst into tears.

Chapter 11

Rosemary couldn't get Hal out of her mind. When he had gone, that Monday morning, she walked for miles along the cliff path, thinking of his face and the way he had looked at her. The more she thought about him, the more guilty she felt.

She tried to talk herself out of it: I know I'm in love with Scott, she thought, but we aren't engaged or anything — and that's his fault, not mine — so surely there's nothing wrong in going to the cinema with Hal. Lots of girls go out with two or three boys at the same time. The advice columns in the magazines tell you to have plenty of boyfriends. And yet she couldn't help feeling uneasy. There was something different about Hal, something sinister, a strange kind of power that both attracted and repelled her. But of course she would meet him at the Roxy; there was no question of opting out. She decided not to tell Leo about it; he'd be horrified if he knew she'd followed him and spoken to Hal.

On her way home to lunch she bought a stick of blue eye shadow in a big store and near the exit she felt a sharp punch in the ribs. She swung around to see Sharon, the girl who lived next door. She looked bigger and tougher than ever and smelled of fish and chips.

"Hello, Rosemary. What have you been buying?" She looked inquisitively at the paper bag in Rosemary's hand.

"Eye shadow. I'm going to the Disco tonight."

Sharon sniffed. "I've seen you two kissing at the garden gate," she said accusingly.

"So what? There's no law against it, is there?"

"You'll have to get him on a diet. He's too fat."

"No, he isn't." Rosemary turned towards the exit, but Sharon followed her.

"He's working at the station, isn't he? As a porter. Don't you mind?"

"Why should I mind?"

"Pretty poor sort of a job — lugging cases about."

"Don't be so snobby, Sharon. It's jolly hard work."

Sharon shrugged. "Oh, well — maybe it'll keep his weight down." Her thin lips curled into a smirk. "I like the look of your *other* bloke, though. Quite a dish, that one."

Rosemary felt her cheeks burning. "What other bloke?"

"The tall fair chap. I saw you with him this morning near the market. Holding hands, too. What would Scott say?"

"We *weren't* holding hands!"

"Yes, you were. I saw you. What's his name, then?"

"None of your business."

"I can ask your brother — I've seen them around together."

"Oh, drop dead!" cried Rosemary. She was trembling with anger.

"That's not very nice, is it? What would your aunt say?"

"I don't care what she'd say." Rosemary turned on her heel and marched out into the street. As she headed for home, she knew that she loved Scott more than ever before; Sharon's remarks had brought it home to her. She thought of him at the station, carrying heavy cases all day in that oppressive heat, and she longed for the evening when she would see him again.

Weekday lunches were never pleasant; Aunt Kay and Uncle Bert dashed in from work for a quick snack and listened to the radio news while Leo and Rosemary ate in silence. On this particular Monday Leo looked as if he'd been crying and hardly touched his food. Rosemary thought he must have had another row with Aunt Kay but she didn't say anything. Hal was right, she thought; boys didn't want their sisters interfering. After lunch he went up to his room and Rosemary decided to spend the afternoon in the garden, improving her suntan.

That night she wore a white dress, with Leo's beads and the new eye shadow. Her skin was golden brown and she knew she looked her best. Scott was waiting outside the Disco, groomed and smart in a blue denim suit.

"Hi, love — you look stunning," he said. "*Extra* stunning." He nuzzled her cheek and turned towards the ticket office.

Rosemary caught his hand. "Scott — let's go somewhere else, can we? Somewhere quiet." She loved the pounding rhythm of disco music, the deafening thump that made talking impossible, but she didn't want that tonight. She wanted to get to know him better, to give him a chance to say that he loved her and that they would always be together.

"Of course — whatever you like," he said. "Coffee bar? Pub?"

"Let's just go down to the harbor."

He put his arm round her waist and they walked slowly through the holiday crowds to the harbor wall. Sitting on the warm stone with the sunset away to their right, they watched the cabin cruisers bump each other gently as the tide came in, their tall masts dark against a delicate coral sky. She thought how blissful it would be to live in one of those little boats with Scott, making curtains for the cabin, cooking in a tiny galley, waking to the sound of the waves and the seagulls.

He said, "Great, isn't it?" and kissed her cheek as if he had known her thoughts.

"Yeah — great." She wanted to talk to him about her longings for the future, to tell him how anxious she was about Leo, even confess about the date with Hal, but the sight of his clear brown eyes, calm and untroubled, made her hesitate. Perhaps there was no need to talk. She would go to the cinema with Hal as arranged, but that would be all; she wouldn't see him again after that. And Leo was tough; he'd be all right . . .

"Like a hamburger?" said Scott. "There's a stall over the road. Bit of a line but it won't take long."

She nodded eagerly. She always felt hungry when she was out with Scott.

He hurried away to the stall and as she waited she fondled the blue beads, looking down at them with pleasure, admiring the vibrant jewel color against her white dress. Poor Leo! She wondered what he was doing that evening. He had so much trouble with Aunt Kay that he spent as much time as possible away from the house. Maybe he was out with Hal again. In The Winner perhaps.

She looked up to see how Scott was getting on in the line but a stream of cars concealed the stall. Then suddenly she heard someone calling her name, and she looked round apprehensively to see who had spoken.

"Rosemary!" It came again but she could see no one she knew, only the strolling holiday-makers and a few boatmen busy with their craft. She squinted into the low sun and then saw Hal, silhouetted against the orange glow of the sky, his hair like copper. Soon he was close beside her, smiling down, his face in shadow. "Hello, gorgeous," he said. "Where's the boyfriend?"

"Gone to get some hamburgers."

"I followed you from the Disco." He sat beside her on the wall.

"Why?" She tried to stare at him calmly but the look in his eyes made her tremble.

"I fancy you," he said. "That's why. I fancy you a lot."

"Don't be silly." She fingered her necklace nervously. "And you'd better get moving — Scott'll be back in a minute."

"What would he say if he saw you with me?"

"How do I know?"

"I'll stick around till he comes back."

"Please yourself." She shifted uneasily.

"Those beads are pretty." He reached out and grasped them, touching her neck at the same time.

"They're the ones Leo bought me. Lovely, aren't they?"

"*You're* lovely. I think I'll kiss you — make your bloke jealous." He tightened his grip on the necklace and pulled her towards him.

"No — please — " She drew away but he held the necklace so firmly that she couldn't escape without breaking it. He kissed her hard and long, hurting her lips, and when he released her Scott was looking down at them. His face was flushed and bewildered as he stood there helplessly, holding the hamburgers. "What's all this?" he said, looking from one to the other.

Hal got up and stared at him insolently. "Is she your property, then?"

Scott shook his head.

"I didn't want him to — " cried Rosemary. "I didn't — "

Hal put out his hand and covered her mouth. "Oh, yes you did," he said. "You wanted it very much."

"I *didn't* — I couldn't get away without breaking the beads!" She clutched the necklace defensively.

"You didn't *want* to get away," said Hal, with his strange mesmeric smile. "But it doesn't matter. Enjoy your hamburgers." He sauntered away, lighting a cigarette, then turned and called out, "See you tomorrow, Rosemary. At the Roxy."

"No, you won't," she cried. "I won't *be* there."

He smiled again. "I'll be waiting." Then he went off into the glare of the sun, tall and straight, the cigarette smoke curling round his head.

"I'm sorry, Scott. Honestly. He asked me to the pictures but I'm not going."

Scott put the hamburgers on the wall but he didn't sit down. "I think you're rotten," he said. "I go across the road for five minutes and look what happens! You make a date with a bloke and let him kiss you — "

"Don't be so childish! It didn't mean a thing — I couldn't help — "

"You made a date with him, didn't you?"

"Yeah, but —"

"But nothing. I thought you were my —"

"Your *property*?"

"No, but I thought you were — were —"

"Were what?" Now her heart was pounding. Perhaps at last he was going to tell her what she wanted to hear.

"Oh, nothing. I just —"

"Sit down, Scott, and let's have our hamburgers."

"You can have them both — I'm not hungry." His voice was unsteady. "And if you want to go to the Roxy with that bloke you can bloody well *go*! He said he'd be waiting."

"I will, then. I *will*." She picked up one of the hamburgers and took a bite out of it. It was greasy and tasteless but she pretended to relish it, chewing steadily, not looking at him.

Scott hesitated and she hoped he would plead with her, but after a while he turned and walked away without a word. She thought, All right, he's asked for it: I really will meet Hal tomorrow night. I'll see that Paul Newman film and have a jolly good time. Why shouldn't I? He's fabulous looking and terribly attractive . . . But in her heart she knew she was deceiving herself. She wanted Scott and no one but Scott. Besides, there was something about Hal that really frightened her.

Chapter 12

That Monday afternoon, Leo sat in his bedroom trying to think of some way out of his terrible dilemma. Rosemary was in the garden, sunbathing. He could see her from his window, lying there in a pink bikini, so pretty and peaceful and unsuspecting, and he felt ill with fear. He wanted desperately to warn her about Hal, to pour out the whole pitiful truth, but he dared not even think of it. It was bad enough to have chickened out of the "baby job"; he couldn't possibly break his oath again by telling Rosemary.

Somehow he'd have to pacify Hal. He'd have to think up a good reason why he hadn't taken the carriage to the boatshed, find Hal, and try to convince him. And he must do it quickly, that very minute . . .

He set off for The Winner, trudging miserably along the scorching streets, racking his brains for an excuse. By the time he arrived he had invented a story; he could only pray that Hal would accept it. The Winner was crowded, as usual, but he found Hal working his favorite pin-table in a far corner.

Leo went and stood beside him. "Hi," he said.

Hal didn't answer. He put another coin in the machine and carried on playing, but Leo knew that he had heard because his jaw was tight and his mouth was hard with anger.

"I — I couldn't help it this morning," began Leo. "You see, the baby — "

Hal swung round suddenly and gave Leo a brutal sideways kick on his ankle.

The pain made him feel sick but it also made him strong and fierce. "Let me *explain!*" he cried. "I just — "

Hal kicked him again, but not so hard. "That sister of yours," he hissed. "She's got it coming to her now. I told you, didn't I?"

"Let me *explain!*" The tears were flooding Leo's eyes so that Hal's demon face became a blur. "The baby wasn't *there!* The woman took it with her into the hut — it wasn't *in* the carriage — "

"That's a lie! I went there and I saw it."

"That was *later* — it wasn't there when *I* went — she took it with her. Honest!" Leo stared at Hal through his wet lashes, willing him to believe it, almost believing it himself, and he felt a glow of relief as he saw by Hal's expression that he was half convinced.

"You're lying," said Hal, "and your sister's going to catch it —"

"Oh, Hal — *no!*" His plea was almost drowned by the laughter and talk around them, the clatter of machines, the drone of traffic outside. The pain in his ankle was getting worse. He didn't know how to cope with the anguish that engulfed him.

Then Hal bent down so that his face was level with Leo's. Leo thought he was going to strike him but he managed to stand straight, without cowering. Hal grabbed him roughly by the arm. "*Unless,*" he said. "*Unless —*"

"Unless what?" Leo waited breathlessly.

"Unless you get me the bread we'd have got from that woman. You bungled it, so you've got to make it up to me."

"All right — I'll get it. How much will it be?" Leo was overwhelmed with relief at this reprieve.

Hal let go of his arm and stood up. "Twenty quid. I reckon that's what we'd have got."

"Twenty! I can't get all that! How *can* I?" Leo was trembling again.

"I don't care how you get it. You'll have to work a job on your own, won't you? Get it by seven o'clock tomorrow night — or else!"

"But — "

"And you'd better make sure of it because I've got a date with that gorgeous sister of yours. How about *that*?"

Leo stared at Hal in horror. Surely he must be lying. "You don't know her," he faltered. "You couldn't have a date with her — you *couldn't* have."

"Ask her, then, if you don't believe me. We're going to the Roxy tomorrow." He gave Leo a push. "Now get out — and you know what'll happen if you don't get that bread."

He turned away and began to play the pintable, leaving Leo to limp away to the exit.

Out in the bright street Leo leaned against a shop window, giddy with pain and anxiety. Twenty quid, he thought. I can't . . . I *can't* . . . Then suddenly he caught sight of a music shop across the road, and in a flash he knew what he must do. He set off for home as fast as his bruised leg would allow him.

Chapter 13

The next morning Rosemary awoke with one of her headaches. She knew it was caused by her quarrel with Scott and her anxiety over the date with Hal, and the more she worried the worse the headache got. She knew that the only cure was peace of mind — to find Scott and tell him she was sorry and that nothing would induce her to go to the Roxy with Hal. But somehow she couldn't do this. Scott would have to make the first move, even though he'd been quite justified in flying off the handle the previous evening. She knew this was unfair, that it was really up to her, but she wasn't strong enough to make the right decision. And so her headache grew worse . . .

It seemed, too, that everything else that morning conspired to upset her. It was raining for the first time in weeks; Leo wouldn't get up, and refused to talk to anyone; Aunt Kay and Uncle Bert argued bitterly all through breakfast about a new deep-freeze that Kay wanted and Bert said they couldn't afford. Kay was still ranting on about it as she left for work.

When the door had slammed behind her, Rosemary and Uncle Bert were alone in the kitchen. He was cleaning his shoes and Rosemary was washing up. The rain lashed the window.

"Nasty wet morning," said Bert. "What are you going to do with yourself today, dear?" He always called her "dear" — and Leo, too — when Aunt Kay wasn't there. Rosemary knew her uncle was very fond of them both.

"Dunno." She suddenly remembered some advice of her father's: *The best way to feel better, if you're ill or depressed, is to make a big effort and start doing something that really interests you. Try to get outside yourself.* Now she decided to do just that. "I think I'll go to the shops to look at some wallpaper books," she said. "Study the latest designs." There were several stores in Brinely with wallpaper departments. They were well supplied with pattern books and you could browse through them for as long as you liked. Nobody seemed to mind if you didn't order anything.

"That's a good idea," said Bert. "It'll help you with your career, won't it?" He had always shown sympathy for Rosemary's ambition to go to an art school and study design. Aunt Kay wanted her to work in a shop and earn some money. "Well, I'll be off now," he said. "Better drag Leo out of bed fairly soon, hadn't you? We don't want him to get into lazy habits."

"He's never been lazy," said Rosemary. "I don't know what's got into him this morning. I'll go up and see."

She laid the table for lunch and then she went up to Leo's room and knocked on the door.

"Who is it?" His voice sounded thick and sulky.

"It's me, pet. Can I come in?"

"If you like."

He was still in bed, a spike of hair and one eye visible from under a mound of untidy bedding. The small room, with its posters and its shelves of toy cars, was dark with rainy gloom. She switched on the light and he vanished completely under the bedclothes.

"Are you all right?" she asked him. "You never stay in bed, do you?"

He exposed two eyes and his nose. "Are you going out soon?" he said.

"Yes — wallpaper shops. Why?"

"When are you going?"

"Soon. What's up — don't you want to be left? I'll stay with you if you like."

He sat up, flushed and wide-eyed. "*No* — I don't *want* you to stay with me. I just — " He broke off and turned away from her.

"You just what?"

"Nothing — I just want to — to be on my *own*."

"All right, I'm going. No need to be huffy. What will you do in the rain? Are you meeting Hal?"

"I might." He got out of bed at the far side and stood looking out of the window, a pathetic little figure in his crumpled pajamas with his hair on end.

Rosemary knew that he wanted her to go, yet somehow she felt she must make contact with him before she left. She thought she might even talk to him about Scott. In the old days they had always told each other their troubles but now there was an uneasy rift between them. She deperately wanted to communicate with him, for his sake as well as hers. It was more important than ever, now that their parents were dead and their aunt and uncle so difficult to talk to.

She hesitated, hoping he would say something himself to break the tension, but he just stood there with his back to her, waiting for her to go.

Suddenly she burst out, "I'm going to the pictures with Hal tonight. Isn't that nice?"

He didn't move but she thought she saw a tremor run through his body.

She went on, "Aren't you surprised?"

He shook his head, and stood there rigidly for a moment, saying nothing. Then suddenly he swung round to face her. His eyes were wild and his face crimson. "Don't go!" he cried. "You mustn't go — *please!*"

"Leo! Don't be so silly. Of course I'm going."

"No — you mustn't — you *mustn't —*"

"Why not? What are you on about, for heaven's sake?"

"He might hurt you —"

"Hurt me? Oh, Leo, what sort of funny ideas have you been picking up? Of course he won't hurt me." Poor little pet, she thought. He's as bad as Uncle Bert — thinks I can't take of myself. He reads the papers and gets worried — not surprising when you think of all the horrible things that *do* happen. She had a sudden memory of Hal's painful grip on her wrist, his savage kiss the night before, the strange glitter of his blue eyes. Maybe she wouldn't meet him after all . . .

"You don't mind me going out with Scott, though, do you?" she said. "You don't think Scott would hurt me?"

"Course he wouldn't! Just go with Scott — don't *ever* go with Hal!"

"I had a fight with Scott last night," she told him. "But I expect we'll make it up." We must, she thought. Must, must, *must* . . .

She looked at Leo's stricken little face and she wondered why he was so much against her seeing Hal. Then suddenly it came to her that he was jealous. Perhaps he felt a kind of hero-worship for Hal and couldn't bear the idea of sharing him. It was understandable.

"Don't go with Hal!" Leo's voice was hoarse with urgency. "If you don't go I'll give you my chemistry set."

"I don't want your chemistry set. I hate chemistry."

"I'll give you anything of mine you want. Honest."

"Look, pet, you can't bribe me — I'll go out with whomever I like. And anyway bribing's beastly. Now get washed and dressed and eat some breakfast. I've left it in the larder."

Leo turned his back on her and sat down on the bed. He said nothing, and she could feel his hostility permeating the room.

"Oh, you're a proper pain, aren't you?" she

cried. "I've got a rotten headache without you making it worse."

He looked at her sourly over his shoulder. "You sound like Aunt Kay."

"Thank you very much — that's all I needed!" She went out, slamming the door, and soon she was hurrying through the rain towards her favorite wallpaper shop. The trouble was, the idea had lost its savor. She couldn't stop worrying. It seemed she was on bad terms with everyone — Aunt Kay, Sharon, Hal, Scott — and now Leo. There was only Uncle Bert, and he was so weak and wishy-washy he hardly counted. She wanted her parents. She wanted Scott. She wanted Scott most desperately . . .

As she trudged through the wet, dismal streets she felt cold inside — cold and hollow, and very lonely.

Chapter 14

As soon as Rosemary was safely out of the house, Leo got dressed, pulling on his clothes in a frenzy of haste. He didn't wash or brush his teeth. For breakfast he gobbled a packet of popcorn he had in the wardrobe. He could think of nothing but the twenty pounds for Hal. But of course it wasn't really for Hal — it was to protect Rosemary.

He could think of only one way of getting the money, and although it sickened his heart he now made his way up the creaking stairs to the attic.

Rosemary had told him about the lute and his uncle had taken him up to look at it one day when Aunt Kay was out. The two of them had spent a happy hour up there, trying to play the instruments. It was the drum Leo liked; the lute didn't excite him. Nevertheless, he remembered Uncle Bert saying it was worth quite a lot of money. It seemed to be his only hope and he consoled himself with the thought that his uncle had a whole attic full of instruments and would hardly miss one.

He hoped — and believed — that no one would suspect him of taking it. There had been several petty robberies in the neighborhood recently so the theft would be easily explained . . .

All these thoughts were vague and jumbled in Leo's mind. He didn't really see much further than the present moment — the imperative need to get the money and save Rosemary. His training in doing "jobs" with Hal had made him more daring and more artful: he went into the attic with the caution and concentration of a practiced burglar.

At first he couldn't find the lute and he began to sweat with fear lest his uncle had sold it or given it away, but at last he discovered it, loosely wrapped in brown paper, on the floor behind a rusty old bird cage. He remembered the pale gold wood and the patterned circle underneath the strings. One day, he thought, he'd make it up to Uncle Bert. He didn't know how, but he *would* . . .

He tucked the lute under his arm, still in

the paper, switched out the light, closed the door and crept downstairs. Even though the house was empty he moved stealthily; it was as if he didn't even want God to see what he was doing. He put on his red hooded windbreaker and went out into the gray downpour. There was nobody about. A dog barked, a window closed next door, but he felt sure that no one had seen him as he started to run towards the town, the big unwieldy parcel clutched under his arm.

He made his way to a small arcade near Hunter's toy shop. He remembered seeing a shop near there with an old harp in the window. It was called "Bargain Antiques" and after hanging about nervously for a while, he took a deep breath and went in. It was a small place, crammed with dark old furniture, stacks of china, silver trays and oddments, a spinning wheel and piles of musty books. When he opened the door a bell rang somewhere at the back, and soon an elderly man appeared. He was bald and pink and wore a blue velvet suit. He smiled and a gold tooth flashed.

"Good morning," he said. "Quite a change in the weather today. Now what can I do for you, sir?"

Leo didn't like the "sir"; it was somehow humiliating. "What'll you give me for this?" he said, handing over the lute.

97

The man took it out of the sodden wrapping paper and examined it from all angles. "Why do you want to sell it?" he said at last.

"I want the money." Leo was trembling, damp all over with perspiration. "I had it given to me," he added breathlessly.

"A legacy, was it?"

Leo didn't know what a legacy was. "Yeah, that's it."

The man took a magnifying glass out of his pocket and studied the lute closely, inspecting every detail. Leo thought, Please God, Please . . .

The man looked up and frowned. "I couldn't offer more than thirty," he said. "How d'you feel about that?"

Leo gulped. "Yeah — well, O.K. — yeah — thanks — " If the man had said a hundred he could hardly have been happier. Rosemary was safe. Even if she went to the cinema with Hal, she was safe. Leo believed this to be true because Hal had proved himself to be reliable, in spite of his vicious ways. Leo hated him but he also respected him.

The man put the lute on a desk and took a pen and a pad of paper out of a drawer. "I'll just take your name and address," he said.

Leo's heart began to thump. "W-why?" he gasped.

"Just a formality." He waited with his pen poised.

There was no escape. "Leo Carter."

The man wrote it down and while he was writing, Leo thought up a false address — a street near his school. "Feather Lane," he said. "Number seven."

The man took a fat wallet from a pocket of his velvet suit and counted out six five-pound notes into Leo's damp, dirty palm. "There you are!" He smiled, showing the gold tooth again. "Don't spend it all at once!"

Leo hurried out of the shop, stuffing the notes into his pocket. He ran all the way to The Winner and when he arrived he was breathless. It was more crowded that usual on account of the rain, but he found Hal at last, leaning over the juke-box, talking to one of his pals. Leo was scared in case he got involved in some terrible new escapade, so he pushed four of the notes into Hal's hand, blurted out, "I got it all right!" and fled.

Out in the street he took the two remaining five-pound notes out of his pocket and gazed at them incredulously. It was more money than he had ever had in his life. Now that Rosemary was safe, he felt a surge of happiness. His uncle might not even notice that the lute had gone; he had so many things up there in the attic, and all in such a muddle. He decided to keep away from Hal for a while. Maybe he'd go round and see Dicky Robertson sometime; he knew where he lived.

Thinking of Dicky Robertson reminded him of the big model racing car he had set his heart on. Suddenly he grunted aloud with excitement, and clutching the ten pounds, he went splashing across the road towards Hunter's.

Chapter 15

When Rosemary arrived home for lunch that Tuesday, Leo was sitting on the floor in the living room, fiddling with a jig-saw puzzle.

"Here you are, pet." She threw him a comic she had bought as a peace offering. She felt much happier now, having decided to go to the railway station that afternoon and make it up with Scott.

"Wow — thanks!" Leo opened the comic eagerly, his face bright with pleasure as he turned to a favorite page.

Rosemary thought, "Blessed are the peacemakers . . . " It must be true because you felt so happy when you made the first move to put things right. It had always been easy to make peace with Leo; he never sulked for long.

"What did you do this morning?" she asked

him. "See Hal?" Talking about Hal was exciting, disturbing, but she had decided not to meet him at the Roxy that night.

"Yeah, but he was with one of his mates. I looked at the shops." He had colored, and she thought, Poor kid — he feels shut out. He shouldn't be so involved with a boy of sixteen. An older friend could be a good influence but a child needs pals of his own age. And anyway she was pretty sure Hal wouldn't have a good influence on anybody. He was hard and selfish and unfeeling — a bully, in fact.

At that moment the door opened and Uncle Bert came in. He smiled at the two of them. "Hello, kids. Your aunt not back yet?"

They shook their heads in unison and Uncle Bert looked relieved. "Rain stopped now," he said. "Everything smells lovely and fresh."

It was pathetic, thought Rosemary, how much happier he looked when his wife wasn't there. No wonder so many of her school friends didn't want to bother getting married if their parents were as miserable together as Bert and Kay. Marriage should be *fun*. It should be warm and sharing, with laughter and kisses and long deep talks. Rows, too, of course, but soon over. With Scott it would be like that; she was sure it would. If you really *wanted* to understand each other you could always work things out. She remembered an old Beatles number called "We Can Work It Out"; John Lennon's voice rang clearly in her mind, and she could hardly wait to get to the station to work things out with Scott.

"I'm just going up to the attic before lunch," said Uncle Bert. "Got a repair job to do. Give me a shout when your aunt comes in."

Leo buried his face in his comic, Uncle Bert vanished upstairs, and Rosemary went into the kitchen to set out the salad for lunch.

Five minutes later Uncle Bert came racing down the stairs as if a mad bull was after him. He burst into the kitchen as Rosemary was eating one of her aunt's chocolate walnuts and she turned away guiltily.

"It's gone!" he gasped. "My lute — it's gone!"

Rosemary faced her uncle, but her mouth was too full of chocolate for her to speak.

"I know just where I left it," he cried. "You haven't been up there, have you? You wouldn't have moved it?"

"No — not for ages. Not since that time you showed me it. Just a sec — I'll ask Leo." She ran into the living room where Leo was still on the floor with his comic. "Leo," she said, "Uncle Bert can't find his lute. You haven't moved it, have you?"

Leo didn't look up. "Course not," he grunted. "Why should I?"

"All *right* — I didn't expect you would have. Poor Uncle Bert — he's frantic."

She went back to the kitchen. Her uncle's face looked paler than ever, the wrinkles deeper and darker. He turned to her eagerly. "Does he know anything? Has he moved it?"

She shook her head. "It must be a burglar, mustn't it? But I always lock up when I go out." She suddenly thought of Leo. Had he forgotten to lock the door that morning? If he had, she'd rather not know about it. After all, the damage was done; it was no use getting him into trouble. And this would surely be enough to make him remember in future.

"Are you going to tell the police?" she said.

"I can't, you see. It's so difficult — your aunt doesn't *know* about the lute — and she'd find out. She wants this deep-freeze and — well, I can't tell her, can I? There'd be an awful row." He ran his fingers through his thin hair. "Could you explain to Leo? Tell him not to say anything — he'll understand. Maybe you could ask next door — ask Sharon if she's seen anyone suspicious."

"I'll go round after lunch," said Rosemary. "Try not to worry, uncle — maybe you'll get it back all right." She heard the front door bang. "Shush — here comes Aunt Kay. I'll just go and tell Leo not to say anything."

* * *

Lunch passed in the usual way, the four of them eating in silence while the news droned over the radio, always depressing, and for Rosemary mostly boring and incomprehensible. There was no other sound but the distant drone of traffic, the twitter of birds in the garden, and the clicking of knives and forks. Rosemary thought how discontented they all looked: Bert gray-faced and drawn, with dull, unhappy eyes; Kay tight-lipped and obviously still resentful about the deep-freeze; Leo strained and withdrawn, his mouth unsteady, as if he was going to burst into tears at any moment. Lord, what a family, she said to herself. And I'm no better; I expect I look as down-in-the-mouth as they do. Still, I'll go and see Scott this afternoon, then everything will be all right. It's *got* to be . . .

Leo excused himself from the table before the others had finished, and went up to his room. Kay said sharply, "What's the matter with *him*? Sour little devil!"

"I don't think he's well," said Rosemary.

"Then he should go to the doctor," said Kay, chewing a radish. Her food never appeared to give her any pleasure.

Bert said, "He's missing his parents, that's his trouble. It's bound to be a bad time for him. For you, too, Rosemary."

105

"Oh, I'm getting over it," she said. She adored her uncle for understanding and decided she would do all she could to get his lute back for him. He loved that lute. If someone had broken in and taken it (and that, she thought, was what *must* have happened), they'd probably try to sell it. She might be able to find it if she did some detective work...

When her aunt and uncle had gone back to work, she went out the front way to see if Sharon was in. Sharon was such a busybody she would be sure to have seen anyone suspicious if she'd been at home.

The gardens were fresh and glittering after the downpour and the sky was blue again. Rosemary rang the next-door bell and was relieved to hear footsteps in the hall. She hoped it was Sharon and not her mother — a big dozy woman who seemed to live in another world.

The door opened and Sharon stood there with a paper dress pattern in her hand. "Hello," she said. "I saw you coming down the path."

"I want to ask you something," said Rosemary. "Something very important."

Sharon frowned suspiciously. "What's up, then?"

"I think we've had burglars."

Sharon's small eyes brightened with curiosity. "Come in," she said.

"No, thanks — I won't stay. The thing is — were you here this morning?"

"Yes — I'm making a dress." She waved the pattern as if to prove she wasn't lying. She prided herself on her needlework, and Rosemary, who couldn't sew a button on without getting the thread into knots, felt a grudging admiration for Sharon's skill.

"Did you see anyone snooping round our house — that's what I wanted to ask you."

Sharon shook her head. "No — what's been stolen?"

Rosemary didn't want to tell her but could hardly refuse when she was asking for help. "A lute of my uncle's. He's got all these musical instruments and some of them are quite valuable. This was really special!"

Sharon frowned, coming forward to lean in the doorway. "You mean one of those things like a mandolin, with a long handle sticking out at a funny angle?"

Rosemary nodded. "Yeah, that's right. Lovely things, they are. My uncle's nuts about them."

"I suppose you know Leo went out with one this morning? I was shutting the window — the rain was coming in — and I saw him with this odd-shaped parcel wrapped in brown paper. There was this handle thing sticking out — with pegs in it, like a guitar. I wondered what it was."

Rosemary felt a cold pain in her stomach. It was as if she had swallowed a great lump of ice, an aching nub of fear that grew more painful every second. She thought wildly, Sharon mustn't know! If it's true — nobody must ever know . . . "Oh, *that*," she said, turning away to hide her distress. "That was another one — Leo was taking it to be mended. Thanks, Sharon — if you didn't see anyone —"

"No — just Leo. And that reminds me — how's the blond boyfriend?"

Rosemary didn't answer and as Sharon laughed and shut the door, she stood for a moment trying to collect her thoughts. It *couldn't* be true — or could it? If Leo had stolen his uncle's lute, he was no longer the straight, sound little boy she had always trusted so implicitly. He was changed, degraded, corrupted. And she could guess who had done it.

But surely there must be an explanation! It *couldn't* be true . . . In any case there was only one way to find out. She gritted her teeth and ran back to the house, racing up the red stairs to Leo's room with prayers and terror in her heart.

Chapter 16

Up in his room, Leo took the model racing car out of its box. His aunt and uncle had gone back to work, Rosemary was out — he had heard the front door slam, and he felt it was safe to have another look at his new toy.

He stroked the shiny green bodywork with a loving finger. He had longed for this car when he first saw it in Hunter's window. Now at last it was his, but oddly there was no real joy in possessing it. He had no one to share it with. He couldn't show it to Rosemary because she would ask him where he got the bread. The very beauty of the car's gleaming bonnet and fat tires, every detail of its exquisite construction, reminded him of his guilt. The car was the same car he had wanted so passionately, but *he* was not the same: Now he hated himself. He put the model back in its box and stuffed it away in the wardrobe.

He picked up the comic which Rosemary had bought him and curled up on the bed. At least she didn't suspect him of taking the lute; he had lied to her and she had accepted it. Of course she had — he hardly ever lied. But what if she found him out? Would she ever be able to trust him again? This round-about of painful thoughts was interrupted by the slam of the front door. Then came the sound of Rosemary's footsteps on the stairs. I hope she leaves me alone, he thought . . .

There was a bang on his door and before he had time to answer, she was there by his bed, her face distorted with anxiety.

"Leo," she cried. "Oh, Leo — what's going on? What were you doing with uncle's lute? Sharon saw you out of the window. Where were you taking it?"

His heart jolted and his cheeks were suddenly on fire. "I never — I didn't — " he began, hiding his face in the comic.

"*Leo*! Tell me th*e truth*! For God's sake — don't lie." She snatched the comic and threw it on the floor. "*Don't lie*!"

He stared at her mutely and the tears came rushing to his eyes. He turned his head away and began to sob, rubbing his wet face with his fists.

"Leo!" She shook him by the shoulder and her nails were sharp and angry through his thin T-shirt. "Leo — *did* you take it? *Did* you?"

He nodded, crying helplessly. He knew there was nothing he could say if Sharon had seen him.

"Did you *steal* it?"

He burst into a new explosion of tears.

"*Did* you?" Her voice was a screech.

"Ye-e-s — go *away* — l-leave me *alone* —"

She gave him a stinging slap across his ear, followed by a violent punch on his back. "You *devil*! You rotten little *devil*! You stole from your uncle — who's been so kind to you. He *loved* that lute! I think you're *horrible* — I *hate* you!" She hit him again, wildly beating at his head and his back and his arm.

Leo scrambled off the bed, out of reach, and stood for a moment, howling with pain and misery. His sister's eyes were hard and unloving, her mouth thin with fury. She had never looked at him like that before, never in all his life.

"What did you do with it?" she cried. "Did you *sell* it?"

He nodded, staring at her through a fog of tears.

"Who to?"

"I don't — r-remember — "

"You do!"

"I don't — I *don't!*" It was true that he didn't remember the name of the shop.

"I'll never forgive you!" Now Rosemary was crying, too. "Never — never! That you could *do* such a thing — and *lie* to me about it — " She lunged at him again and he ducked away from her, hurling himself out of the room.

He didn't wait to see if she was following him; he raced down the stairs, out of the back door and down the road as fast as he could go. He only wanted to escape from her anger and her blows, never to have to face that look of hatred, that battering of abuse. I can't go back, he thought — I can't *ever* go back . . . He went on running, limping with his bruised ankle, searching blindly for somewhere to hide.

Chapter 17

The more she thought about it, the more remorseful Rosemary felt about the way she had hit Leo and the dreadful things she had said to him. She hadn't even given him a chance to explain.

When he ran out of the house she didn't follow him — she was too angry, too sick, too overcome with tears — but after a while she went for a walk, hoping to find him in the town. She looked in The Winner without success; she wandered up and down the crowded Promenade; at last she gave up and escaped from the press of people onto a dirty patch of beach littered with refuse and smelly seaweed. No one was there except a woman with untidy gray hair who wandered along collecting driftwood in a sack.

Rosemary sat down on a rock and tried to decide what to do. One thing was certain: She wasn't going to give Leo away. At tea-time she would cuddle him up, say how sorry she was, and promise never to tell. Even Scott mustn't know, although she longed to rush to the station to ask for his help. She must cope on her own. She must find out what had driven Leo to do such a thing. She felt sure that Hal was behind it, and she shivered, thinking of his charm and its underlying menace. She remembered Leo's passionate entreaty: "Don't go — he'll hurt you." Supposing it was true! Whatever happened, she must persuade Leo to tell her everything.

The woman with gray hair came trudging by, dragging her sack of wood, her bare feet black with sludge. She smiled at Rosemary as she passed, and it was a warm gentle smile, the kind that gives you courage, even when it comes from a stranger you might never see again.

"Hello," said Rosemary. The greeting came spontaneously: she just wanted to make contact.

"Hello, love!" The woman's smile widened. Her wrinkled eyes were bright and her cheeks fat and shiny. She paused, putting down the sack. "You look a bit sad," she said. "Is anything the matter?"

Rosemary looked up at her and a flash of understanding seemed to run between them, a current of sympathy and love. This woman was suddenly a sort of mother to her and she longed to pour out her distress and ask for comfort and advice. Yet somehow she couldn't bring herself to do it. She couldn't talk. It was as if the words were trapped, as they had been on that terrible day when she heard about the air crash on the radio.

She shook her head and looked away, blinking at the dazzle of the sea. The woman waited a moment and then she picked up her sack and went on her way. She turned and called out, "Bye-bye, dear. God bless!"

"Good-bye," murmured Rosemary. She watched her climb the stone steps to the Promenade and then she set off for home. It was nearly tea-time. Leo would be back, and she could hardly wait to find out the whole story, to comfort him, and to make him promise — whatever happened — to keep away from Hal.

"Where's Leo?" Aunt Kay was frying sausages and Rosemary was setting the supper table. Leo hadn't come home for tea. Now it was nearly seven o'clock and there was still no sign of him.

"Dunno. Out."

"I *know* he's out. I've been shouting all over for him."

"He'll be back soon — he always turns up for his food." Rosemary looked anxiously out the window. She ached for the sight of that stocky, ginger-headed little figure stumping up the path. Suppose he was too frightened to come home because of the row they'd had. She'd never hit him like that before, never said she hated him . . .

"Where's your uncle?" said Kay.

"Up in the attic."

"That *blasted* attic! He's never here when he's wanted."

"What do you want him for?"

"To open this can of peas. It hurts my wrist." She flung down the opener and rubbed her wrist irritably.

"Give it to me — I'll do it." Rosemary opened the can and put the peas in a pan to heat.

Kay gave her one of her rare smiles. "You're a good girl, aren't you? Your mother'd be proud of you. I wish I could say the same for Leo."

"He's lovely, really," said Rosemary, stirring the peas. "Just a bit wild."

"Like his father — that's *his* trouble."

"Don't say anything against Daddy — please —"

"I'll say what I choose, Rosemary, without instructions from you. I'm just about —"

The door opened and Bert came in. "Supper ready?" he asked. His face looked grayer and sadder than ever.

"Yes it is, but no thanks to you," said Kay. "And Leo isn't back yet."

Rosemary said, "He's been out since two o'clock."

Kay served out sausages and chips for the three of them. Rosemary added the peas, leaving some in the pan. "What about Leo's supper?" she said. "You haven't left him any."

"He can do without," snapped Kay. "If he can't be on time he can go hungry."

Rosemary felt the start of one of her headaches. "He can have mine, then!" she cried. Oh, why did her aunt have to be so anti-Leo!

"No, he can't. Just you sit down and eat it."

"I don't want any."

"Sit down and *eat* it, I said! I shan't give it to Leo in any case."

"No!" Rosemary snatched up her bag "I'm going out to look for him. He might be *hurt* for all we know. I think you're *horrible*, Aunt Kay."

"Now, now," said Bert. "You mustn't say anything —"

But Rosemary heard no more. She was out of the door and on her way to the back gate. As she hurried down the road, a distant clock struck seven. Suddenly she remembered her date with Hal. He might be waiting for her at that very moment. Her heart began to throb with a fearful excitement and she knew she must go and see if he was there. She might be able to find out where Leo was and why he had stolen the lute.

She stopped to open her bag, and after putting on a gloss of bright lipstick and running a comb through her hair, she set off in the direction of the Roxy cinema.

Chapter 18

Leo ran until he was choking with exhaustion. His body smarted from Rosemary's slaps and punches but it was his mind that suffered most. He was crushed and terrified by what she had said: *"I'll never forgive you . . . I hate you . . ."* The words burned with an agonizing power and with every step he took he became more certain that he couldn't go back to the house that night. He felt he could never go back.

He raced down deserted back streets to the suburbs. He ran along the edge of an empty football ground, across muddy fields, through a derelict railway station. Then, lost and frightened, he made his way back to the town, taking a church spire as his guide. He didn't know where to go: He only knew he must escape from Rosemary, from Uncle Bert, from Hal, from the police. Most of all — though he could hardly comprehend it — he wanted to escape from himself.

At last he came to the entrance of the car dump where Scott had buried the dog. It was a relief to know where he was — only half a mile or so from home — and he went in, heading for the familiar blue car. It was only just over three weeks since that evening when the policeman had taken Scott's name in his notebook, but it seemed like months. So much had happened, so many terrors and miseries had occupied his mind, and all because of Hal.

No one was about. The long rows of abandoned cars glinted in the sunlight and the grass was still wet with the morning's rain. Leo made his way to the dog's grave behind the car. On the freshly turned soil he could see the remains of the roses. The leaves and blooms were withered and brown but the thorny stalks lay criss-crossed on the moist earth. He'd been wrong to think it was silly of Rosemary to bring the flowers. It wasn't silly at all — it was a beautiful idea. He pictured the dog lying underneath; its bones would be there for years — perhaps forever. He wondered if dogs went to heaven. He thought they must, because they never did any harm except by instinct, which they couldn't help. *People* did. Hal did . . . and Aunt Kay . . .

Suddenly he caught sight of some men passing the entrance to the dump and in a panic of fright he wrenched open the rear door of the car and scrambled inside, shutting it behind him. There was a musty smell of leather and decay. The upholstery was damp where the rain had come in through a gap in the window but he huddled on the seat, keeping well out of sight. He felt like a criminal; he *was* a criminal — and he had given his name to the man in the antique shop. Sooner or later the police would be sure to catch him, but how could he tell them the truth without danger to Rosemary . . . He let out a moan of torment as he thought of Hal's threats. He must never tell — never. The worst that could happen to him would be a detention center and that couldn't be much more horrible than living with Aunt Kay.

He lay there, stiff and aching, afraid to get out of the car in case he was seen. He would have given anything for a can of Coke and a hamburger. There was plenty of money in the pocket of his jeans, left over from the racing car, but he dared not go to the shops to buy food.

The sun dipped behind the trees, making rainbow colors in the dirty glass of the windshield. A blackbird was singing. Traffic droned in the distance. Leo shivered. The car seat was clammy and chilly through his thin T-shirt and he hugged himself for warmth as the evening light glittered through the leaves and finally vanished.

There was a long, lonely period of dusk and at last the sky grew dark. Car headlights flashed intermittently, catching the car mirror, lighting up the stained backs of the front seats. He was trembling with cold, too sick and exhausted even to cry, and gradually he became aware of a single star winking away in the blackness. Through the bleary windshield it seemed near and friendly; it comforted him as the eye of the gull had done that day on the cliffs. *That day on the cliffs* . . . But it was only *yesterday*! He closed his eyes, stupefied by the confusion of his life since Hal had taken it over. There was no more order in his days; time was a crazy jumble of fear and misery. It suddenly came to him that Hal was like a gangster who terrorized innocent people to get more money for himself. One day, if he wasn't stopped, Hal might be a *real* crook, bribing and blackmailing and killing people.

If he wasn't stopped . . . It was too frightening, too difficult, and after a while Leo turned over on the narrow seat, curled himself up, and fell asleep.

Chapter 19

Hal was waiting in the cinema foyer where a line was forming at the box office. He wore a heavy blue shirt and white slacks, and he was smoking a small cigar. "I knew you'd come." His smile was sardonic.

"I nearly didn't," said Rosemary, "but I wanted to ask you a few things."

He came and stood very close to her, toying with the lacy collar of her dress. "I still fancy you," he said.

She was tense with nerves but she spoke as coolly as she could. "Don't be funny — my brother's in trouble and I've got to find out about it."

"What kind of trouble?"

"I don't really know. He's been — "

"Smashing eyes you've got, Rosemary." He turned towards the box office. "Circle or stalls?"

"Neither, thanks. I'm not coming in."

"Oh, yes you are!" He glared at her angrily.

"No, I'm not — I've got to *talk* to you! *Please!*"

He sighed audibly, drew on his cigar, then switched on a charming smile. "All right — you win. What can I do when a pretty girl says please?" He took her arm and led her out into the sunny street. "Now what's all this about?" he said in a friendly tone.

"Where can we go to talk?"

"That doorway over there."

They crossed the road to the entrance of a camera shop. The shop was closed and they stood in the quiet alcove beside an array of photographic equipment.

Rosemary said, "Leo's been stealing and I —"

"*Stealing?*" Hal's blue eyes opened wide. He looked both surprised and concerned. "Has he *really?* That's bad, isn't it? What's he been up to — shop-lifting?"

"No, he's stolen a lute from his uncle. I thought you might know something about it?"

"*Me?* Why should *I* know?"

"Well, you've been with him a lot, haven't you?" Rosemary was beginning to feel embarrassed. "I mean I thought — "

"I can't help it if he hangs around, can I?" Hal relit his cigar, blowing clouds of aromatic smoke into Rosemary's face. "I tell him to clear off but he won't go and I don't like to hurt his feelings. Can't he find some friends of his own age?"

"I wish he would — but I didn't want to interfere."

"I'll tell him myself if I see him. Now how about this film? Come on — there's still time." He took her hand.

"Hal, I can't." Rosemary wished she didn't have to refuse. He'd obviously been sweet to Leo and she was sure he had nothing to do with the lute affair. "He didn't come home for his supper and he's never stayed out before. We had a terrible row and I'm worried about him. I must go back and see if he's there."

"Nonsense — he isn't a baby."

"He is though, in some ways. I'm sorry — I *must* go back."

Hal shrugged. "O.K. I'll go to the pictures by myself." He puffed moodily at the last of his cigar and threw it away. "Don't take any notice if Leo tells you a pack of lies about me," he said. "He might feel sore because I didn't want him around."

Rosemary shook her head. "He wouldn't do that — he thinks a lot of you."

Hal put his hands on her shoulders and kissed her firmly on the lips, a deep, searching kiss that left her breathless. "See you," he said at last. "And tell that kid brother of yours to remember all the things I've told him."

She watched Hal stroll across the road to the cinema and then she set off for home. She thought, How could I have been so wrong about him? Of course, he's got a savage streak, but so have I. Look at the way I went for Leo . . .

She hurried homewards and on the way she bought some sandwiches for Leo's supper. Surely he would be home by now.

Uncle Bert was mowing the front lawn. He beckoned her into a corner of the garden.

"Is Leo back?" she said.

"No — not a sign. But I'd like a word with you." He looked anxiously at the house. "Your aunt's in the kitchen. She mustn't know about this."

Rosemary thought, Whatever's coming? Her uncle's face was twitching with nerves.

"I've been talking to Sharon," he said. "She saw Leo going out with my lute this morning — she told you, didn't she? And you said he was getting it repaired."

Rosemary groaned. It hadn't occurred to her that her uncle might talk to Sharon as well. So the secret was out!

He went on, "I can see why you said that — and why you didn't tell me. You thought he'd stolen it, didn't you?"

"He *did* steal it," said Rosemary.

"No — no, he didn't. You see, I *gave* it to him. I'd forgotten — it completely slipped my mind, but I said he could have it weeks ago. He didn't seem to want it."

Rosemary stared at her uncle and she knew that he was lying; he was lying to save face for Leo. In a flash she also knew that she must pretend to believe him.

"That's great," she said. "I really thought he'd pinched it. What a relief!"

"So you won't be angry with him, will you? It's bad enough with your aunt — she doesn't understand."

Rosemary wasn't going to tell Uncle Bert about her row with Leo. "I've got some sandwiches for his supper," she said, waving the paper bag. "Cheese and tomato."

"Good — he'll be hungry." He looked down at his hands. "I wish your aunt didn't — make things — difficult," he said in a low voice.

"So do I. But *you* don't, uncle. And that's a big blessing for us."

He glanced up at her and the change in his face was like a miracle; he looked ten years younger, all in a second.

She went up to Leo's room and decided to hide the sandwiches in his wardrobe, so Aunt Kay couldn't find them. Just as she was closing the wardrobe door, she caught sight of a brightly colored cardboard box at the back, behind his football boots. She picked it up and looked inside at the brand-new racing car. The price was written on the box — £6.95.

My God, she thought, What's *happening*? Oh Leo — whatever's got into you? It was Aunt Kay's fault for stopping his pocket money, for not understanding about Sunday School, for being so unkind . . .

Rosemary stood with the box in her hand for a long time and suddenly she knew what she must do. She must find Scott. She must tell him everything and ask him to help her. He was studying sociology, training to become a probation officer. He would know what to do.

She decided to go to his house. She'd never been there but the address had been stamped on her mind ever since that first day at the car dump, when the policeman had written it in his notebook.

She put the box back in the wardrobe, took out her lipstick and scrawled "*Leo, I love you*" on his wardrobe mirror.

Then she ran out of the house and headed for Marine Street. Her tiff with Scott was almost forgotten; it was Leo that mattered. Somehow he must be found — and quickly, before it got dark.

Chapter 20

Leo was awakened by a tapping on the car window. He let out a squeal of fear, but a moment later he heard a familiar voice. "It's all right — it's me — Scott!"

"Scott — oh, Scott — " Leo sat up, almost crying with relief. The car door creaked and Scott was there in a big red jersey, his face round and smiling in the clear moonlight.

"Move over," he said, climbing into the car. "We'll sit in here for a bit and you can tell me all about it."

"Where's Rosemary?" Leo was shivering uncontrollably.

"She stayed at home in case you came back. She said if I found you to tell you she didn't mean *any* of the things she said this afternoon. She said, 'Tell him I love him more than ever.' "

Leo began to cry and Scott put a hefty arm round his shoulders. "Hey, you're frozen," he cried. "Here — have my sweater." He peeled it off and helped Leo to struggle into it. It was warm and thick and twice his size. He hugged himself into it like a blanket, still trembling.

"Listen, Leo," said Scott gravely, "you'll have to tell me *everything* if I'm going to help you. *Everything.*"

"I — I can't. I promised not to — "

"Who did you promise? Hal?"

He nodded.

"I thought it might be that," said Scott. "And he's threatened you, hasn't he? Threatened to hurt Rosemary?"

Leo stared at him in amazement. "How did you know that?"

"She told me you'd implored her not to go out with him. She thought it was because you were jealous — "

"I wasn't jealous," protested Leo. "He said he'd beat her up — he said he'd — he'd — "

"He'd what?"

"He said he'd grind a broken bottle into her face — that's what he said." Leo felt better for voicing at last the terror that had haunted him since he had sworn on his own blood never to tell.

Scott winced. "Oh, Leo," he said, "we've got to get Hal into custody, you know that, don't you? He mustn't get away with it. You'll have to tell me everything, right from the start. But not tonight."

"I stole my uncle's lute."

"He told Rosemary he gave it to you."

"He didn't — he *didn't*. He mustn't say that. I *stole* it — to get the twenty pounds for Hal. We must get it back for him." He wiped his eyes on a fold of Scott's jersey. "I can show you the shop."

"We'll do that tomorrow, don't worry. And we'll tell the police about Hal."

"What'll they do to him?"

"Depends. Depends on his record — and his background. Do you know about his parents?"

"His father drinks a lot, he says. He hasn't got a mother."

Scott opened the car door. "Come on — let's get you home. They're all worried sick about you. It's nearly one o'clock."

When he stood on the grass outside the car, Leo found that Scott's jersey hung below his knees and his hands were half way up the sleeves.

"Can't wear this," he muttered, struggling out of it. Scott put the jersey on again and as he waited, Leo caught sight of the side mirror hanging at an angle where Scott had wrestled with it that first Sunday. In a moment he was tugging at it with all his might, wrenching and heaving as if his life depended on it. Suddenly it broke away, pulling with it a rusted lump of the car.

"Here you are, Scott!" He waved it in triumph. "Here's that mirror you wanted! I've got it for you!"

Scott took it and held it up to the moonlight, pretending to admire himself. "Thanks a lot, Leo. This is my lucky day. Getting this — and finding you!"

"How did you guess where I was?" asked Leo, as they walked towards the road.

"I don't really know. It was a kind of hunch. I suddenly *knew* — just as if you were calling me."

Leo chuckled. "P'raps I *was* — in my sleep. I had some awful dreams."

Scott put his arms round Leo's shoulders. "You'll have to be tough, you know. You'll have to give evidence in court. It won't be easy, but it's got to be done. If you know something's wrong you must always battle against it."

Leo nodded. He wasn't afraid, with Scott on his side.

They walked in silence through the dark deserted streets and there was only the sound of their footsteps—Scott's long and slow, Leo's shorter and quicker, to keep up.

At last Leo said, "Scott, are you going to marry Rosemary?"

He didn't answer at once. A car went by, lighting up the great mass of his red jersey, his thick black hair, the rosy curve of his cheek.

Then he spoke very quietly, his voice hardly audible against the sound of their footsteps. "I hope so," he said. "One day."

"Good," said Leo, kicking a stone along the moonlit road. "*I* hope so, too."

Chapter 21

"Now just go to sleep and don't *worry*," said Rosemary. She stood by Leo's bedroom door, her hand on the light switch. He was lying on his back and she gazed anxiously at his pale face, the dark shadows under his eyes, the trembling, tragic little mouth.

"I c-can't *help* worrying," he whimpered, and a tear rolled out of his eye corner and soaked into the pillow.

"You'll feel better in the morning. Everything's going to be all right. We'll get the lute back — and Hal won't know what's hit him when the police get moving. Now go to sleep, pet. It's nearly two o'clock."

"Where's Scott?"

"Down in the living room — sitting on the sofa with Aunt Kay, drinking tea."

"I *hate* her!"

"I know, but she's sorry — she really is. She says you can have all the pocket money you missed in a lump sum."

"I don't want it."

"Yes, you do. You can put it in your savings box. Now good night."

Leo turned on his side and looked at Rosemary with wide bright eyes. "I *love* Scott," he said.

Rosemary thought, So do I — oh, golly, so do I! She said, "Yeah, he's great, isn't he?"

"I got him that side-mirror — I pulled it off the car."

"He showed it to me. Good for you." She turned out the light and closed the door, eager to get downstairs and be with Scott.

He was still sitting with Kay on the sofa. Bert was collecting the empty teacups on to a tray. Rosemary sat on the edge of the table and looked at Scott, lounging there in his red jersey, looking perfectly at ease. She loved him so much that her whole body ached with it.

Aunt Kay said, "Don't sit on the table, dear — you'll weaken the joints."

Rosemary sighed and flopped onto the carpet at Scott's feet. She wanted to lean against his knees but she didn't know whether he had forgiven her for making that date with Hal. They hadn't had a chance to make up their quarrel, only to talk about finding Leo. He might even have another girl friend by now . . .

Kay stood up, smoothing her dress. "I can't understand this Leo business at all," she said irritably. "He seemed happy enough."

"No, he didn't," snapped Rosemary. "I knew he wasn't happy. I knew there was something wrong and I jolly well ought to have found out what it was. I ought to have made him tell me all about that bloody Hal, right from the start."

"Don't use that word," said Kay.

"He'd promised not to tell," said Scott. "And besides he was scared to death on your account. So don't blame yourself too much."

"Well, I *do*," said Rosemary. "I should have taken more care of him."

Bert said, "Come on — it's time we were all in bed."

Scott picked up the side-mirror from the sofa beside him, and got to his feet. A chunk of rust fell off it onto the carpet and Kay retrieved it, frowning with distaste, and put it onto the tray with the teacups. Rosemary suppressed a giggle and made a loud snorting noise instead. Her uncle gave her a gentle look of admonition.

Scott said to Bert, "I'd like a walk round

the block with Rosemary before I go, if that's all right with you?"

Rosemary's heart began to thump. She wanted desperately to be alone with him but she was terrified in case he didn't want her any more.

Kay sniffed. "It's two o'clock in the morning," she exclaimed. "Much too late."

"It's rather important," pursued Scott steadily.

"What are the neighbors going to think?" went on Kay. "Seeing our girl with a — with a man — at this time of night?"

"They're all in bed asleep," said Bert drily, "so they won't think anything at all." He smiled at Scott. "Don't be too long, will you? We'll go on up, Rosemary. Mind you lock the door when you come in." He turned to his wife. "We've got a lot to thank Scott for," he reminded her. "Finding Leo like that."

"We're very grateful, I'm sure," said Kay stiffly. Rosemary thought, she finds it really hard to say anything nice. Maybe it was something she just couldn't help . . .

"Come on, Scott," she said, and led the way out into the cold, moonlit street.

They walked in silence to the corner, their blue-black shadows moving ahead of them, not touching, their footsteps loud on the deserted pavement. When they were out of sight of the house, Rosemary said, "Now, what's so important?" Her voice sounded cool and off-hand but she was trembling with nerves.

They were passing a telephone box and Scott took her hand. "Let's go in here," he suggested. "It'll be cosier. There's something I've got to tell you."

In the dimly-lit kiosk they stood face to face and she was afraid he would hear her heart beating. He put his arms round her and kissed her gently on the forehead.

"What is it, then?" she muttered. She looked down at the floor, still uncertain about him. It was littered with spent matches and cigarette butts, a sickening reminder of Hal. The air smelled of stale tobacco.

"It's this," said Scott. "I love you. One day I want to marry you."

The tears rushed into her eyes. "So do I!" she gasped. "Oh, Scott, so do I!" She flung her arms round his neck and buried her face against his shoulder, weeping with joy.

He said, "I think I must have been in love with you since that very first day."

"Me too."

"I couldn't *bear* it when I saw you with Hal like that."

"I'm sorry —"

"No — I should have knocked his block off. I should have stuffed those hamburgers down his rotten throat."

"Before you knocked his block off — or after?"

They laughed hysterically, clinging together and kissing each other in a frenzy of love and relief.

At last she said, "Why did you want to tell me tonight?"

"Because I told Leo and I was afraid he might tell you himself before I had a chance to."

Rosemary drew away from him, banging her elbow on the telephone. "You told *Leo*?" Her passion had suddenly turned to indignation. "Whatever did you tell *him* for?"

"He asked me. He said on the way home tonight, 'Are you going to marry Rosemary?'"

"And what did you say?"

"I said I hoped so."

"What did he say to that?"

"He said he hoped so, too." He stroked her cheek. "You look fabulous in the moonlight."

"You look fabulous in that red jersey."

He grinned. "I suppose I'd better see you home, now. We've had our ten minutes."

Rosemary didn't move; she just went on gazing at him. "When we're married," she said, "you'll be Leo's brother. He'll *love* that!"

"So will I," said Scott. And he kissed her again.